BLINDSIGHT

A NOVEL

Maurice Gee

PENGUIN BOOKS

PENGUIN BOOKS

Published by the Penguin Group

Penguin Group (NZ), cnr Airborne and Rosedale Roads, Albany, Auckland
1310, New Zealand (a division of Pearson New Zealand Ltd)

Penguin Group (USA) Inc., 375 Hudson Street, New York, New York 10014, USA

Penguin Group (Canada), 10 Alcorn Avenue, Toronto, Ontario, Canada M4V 3B2
(a division of Pearson Penguin Canada Inc.)

Penguin Books Ltd, 80 Strand, London, WC2R 0RL, England

Penguin Ireland, 25 St Stephen's Green, Dublin 2, Ireland (a division of
Penguin Books Ltd)

Penguin Group (Australia), 250 Camberwell Road, Camberwell, Victoria 3124,
Australia (a division of Pearson Australia Group Pty Ltd)

Penguin Books India Pvt Ltd, 11, Community Centre, Panchsheel Park,
New Delhi - 110 017, India

Penguin Books (South Africa) (Pty) Ltd, 24 Sturdee Avenue, Rosebank,
Johannesburg 2196, South Africa

Penguin Books Ltd, Registered Offices: 80 Strand, London, WC2R 0RL, England

First published by Penguin Group (NZ), 2005
3 5 7 9 10 8 6 4 2

Designed and typeset by Egan-Reid Ltd
Printed in Australia by McPherson's Printing Group

ISBN 0 14 302023 4
A catalogue record for this book is available from the
National Library of New Zealand.

www.penguin.co.nz

PENGUIN BOOKS

BLINDSIGHT

Maurice Gee is one of New Zealand's best-known writers, for both adults and children. He has won a number of literary awards, including the Wattie Award, the Deutz Medal for Fiction, and the New Zealand Fiction Award. He has also won the New Zealand Children's Book of the Year Award. In 2003 he received an inaugural New Zealand Icon Award and in 2004 he received a Prime Minister's Award for Literary Achievement.

Maurice Gee's novels include the *Plumb* trilogy, *Going West*, *Prowlers*, *Live Bodies* and *The Scornful Moon*. He has also written a number of children's novels, the most recent being *The Fat Man*, *Orchard Street* and *Hostel Girl*.

Maurice lives in Wellington with his wife Margareta, and has two daughters and a son.

ONE

Father taught us how not to love.

The thought came fully formed as my brother walked by. As usual he did not see me, for I never stand in his way, but he slowed his step and changed his line for others on the footpath: college girls in summer uniforms, office workers with swipe cards on their belts. The girls look away with that affronted expression the young, especially the female young, take on at the sight of dereliction and decay. They cannot believe in a fall of such magnitude and set their faces in hostility. Some of the office workers believe. A man, well dressed, said: 'Gidday, mate.' That was kind of him – or perhaps it expressed foreknowledge in some way. Gordon did not hear; but must, I believe, have heard the whispering in my head, the message, the reminder, from the sister he had loved.

I wanted to say it aloud: 'Gordon, Father taught us . . .', not to plead with him for recognition but to explain our lives, or at least make the attempt. He would not have understood. And, indeed, it's ambiguous. But I mean Father's greediness in love, his benevolence and appetite, which started Gordon and me on our divergent ways.

This is how we come together: Alice walking up Molesworth Street and Gordon walking down. He hears no message, even when I add to it: I love you, Gordon, not in Father's way, and I thank you, take care – which is the silliest thought I could ever have.

I don't blame Father – who owns that name (the fellow up in heaven can't compete) and usually owns 'he' and 'him' as well. The other men I've known stand aside, although Gordon and Neville have places more important in their way. My secondary list – Tom, Derek, Fergus, Jake, and Richie of course – is too long for decency, but I was trying hard to get rid of and to find, not simply bed-hopping in the modern way. I talked the matter over with Gordon one day but went too far and he protested: 'For God's sake, Sis!' He told me to get my hooks in the lawyer one and marry him. That was a slap in the face. I'd have gone to bed with my brother if he'd asked me, or touched me, or if he'd even hinted at a need; but it would have been ruinous, for in those days he used me as a kind of fixed star, far away, glittering, unchanging and pointing him along the way to go; but a star close at hand as well, that he could pluck down and slide into his pocket to keep him warm. Pointing his way, keeping him warm, were sisterly acts, and the needs that he once or twice told me of, and at other times nudged me to understand, could only be satisfied by a lover – with whom I became fierce in advance, instructing her.

There's nothing dark in this, just too much closeness, too much love, and love goes back to Father, doesn't it?

We were a happy family, like in those cards: Mr Bun and Mrs Bun and the two Bun children. We rested on a ground of love, and also of pride in what I'll call our Ferry-ness, and no holes opened underneath. I could write our childhood tale: a kitcheny mother, a father who completed us, coming home from work. We felt no need for a dog or cat. We had puddings, games, stories, sunburned salty holidays at Brown's Bay, long cosy winters by the fire, and when the year ended we carried home school reports in brown envelopes, which Mother leaned against the mantelpiece clock for Father to open when he came home. Then we saw his throat swell with pride and his face redden with pleasure. *Excellent, Excellent*, Gordon's report said. He rarely sank to my level of *Very Good*.

But I'm not going to do it: Father, Mother (notice I don't say Mum and Dad), the beach, the kitchen, playgrounds, reports, because I don't want to, it's as simple as that. I'm not afraid of what I'd find. There's nothing to be afraid of in those bedrooms and that living-room, in the garden, in the street, in our town.

The full flow of emotions, that is what I choose. How wonderful it was. The caring for each other, the comforting. Perhaps I should add, the eating up, for I was full of Father and Mother and Gordon, and they of me. There was nothing wrong with it, but I'm trying, I am trying, to see what was right, beyond the ease and comfort and fullness of it all. I'm trying to see the world and other people beyond our fire, in the dark.

We extended our benignity out there, and Father, Mother too, had sensible knowledge of friends and neighbours, I am sure; but I saw faces that must either frown or smile, and Gordon, he's never said, but was it – I try to fit my mind into his – ghostly suppliants? He stepped out into the world with such innocence and goodwill.

Here's a tale: it is 1942, or is it 43? Anyway, the time of battles in the desert overseas and our brave boys halting the madman Hitler in his tracks and just beginning to push him back. Father is too old to go to the war but Mother is beginning to ask, Will it all be over . . .? She means before Gordon is old enough to go. Gordon is ten. That is the sort of worry excessive love can breed. She is bosomy, our mother, apron-wrapped, floury-handed, professionally cheerful and deeply worry-fraught. There is so much out in the world to damage us. It seems designed for such a purpose: an outside world made for killing children. In our town, in our years at primary school, a boy – our paper-boy – fell under the train at Loomis station, and two sisters from the Catholic school drowned in the creek (they were found locked in each other's arms, which thrilled me and made me weep: I could do both things at once). These tragedies confirmed Mother in her belief that death fell in behind us when we stepped outside our door, and she laid charmed phrases on us as we set off for school: 'Stay on the footpath. Remember to look both ways.' And: 'Don't go near the creek, promise me. God bless.' She still believed in God, although I can't recall any other time she appealed to him.

We started off along our street, past the railway houses, with our leather schoolbags on our backs and lunches wrapped in newspaper inside – brown bread spread with Marmite and peanut butter and honey – and crossed the bridge down in the hollow, climbed to the road running beside the railway line, passed the jam factory and Ah Lap's store – but I remind myself I'm not doing the childhood bit, with its memory of contentment and warmth, with its details of bread, jam, apples, milk at school, superannuated teachers back to take the place of men gone to the war, spelling ('i' before 'e' except after 'c'), mental arithmetic, long division, and the strap for boys 'as stupid as Russian peasants' who can't name all the countries coloured red on the map. See how easily I force myself. What does it prove? That we had a childhood? That my memory is OK? I don't want these things, but to deal in mystery. I want to know how Gordon came to be and where he has travelled and where his memory has gone. I don't believe it has broken up over the years and faded to nothing like a cloud, but hold the wishful image of a sunken ship lying intact on the ocean floor, waiting to be found and raised. If I can make him see me and if he can find my name . . . I practise all sorts of things to say.

So – 1942 or 43. Our side of the street is the high side. You climb a dozen steps cut in the bank to reach our path. Five railway houses lie on the other side, above the abandoned orchard and the swamp. A signalman, a driver, three track workers live there, men too old for the war. The Catholic Boyles are at the end of the line, beside an arm of the swamp that runs along the road edge. Father and Mother have seen the four Boyle boys grow up – ragamuffins, Father says; hooligans, says Mother – and seen them go two by two into the army. Now Mike, the oldest one, is dead.

We, the Ferrys, are respectful and hushed. We stand at our front windows and watch the priest go in, and I wish, romantically, that we had a priest, but then see it as a wish that one of us will die. I mew with fright and Mother reaches out her arm and hugs me to her side.

'I've written them a letter,' Father says. 'I've told them how we all – Alice and Gordon, you too ...' He fits his hand caplike on my head and his other hand on Gordon's. We project waves of sorrow and comfort over the street at the Boyles' house and the Boyles inside.

I must stop writing in that tone. Simply, it's not fair. Father's sorrow was genuine. No matter how hard I try, with Mike Boyle's death and everything else, I cannot catch him out in pretence. He meant what he said, and what he did. In the Boyles' case he wrote his letter of condolence and carried it across the road to put in their box the following morning on his way to work. I liked the thought of my name being there. Tears filled my eyes as he slid it into the wooden mouth. Previously 'killed in action' had been exciting. Father created new feelings in me.

We sang *God Save the King* and saluted the flag and marched class by class into school. My room was Standard Five, Gordon's Four (he skipped a year). The spelling and arithmetic and strapping began. There was also art. Mr Warren was teaching us perspective, and I drew our family in the foreground and unnamed people, pigmy-sized then doll-sized then as small as mice, farther off. It was like a chart of human evolution with the Ferrys showing how far the human race had advanced.

Gordon, with Miss Grandison, had drawing too. His picture lay flat. (Standard Four hadn't learned perspective.) He posted it in the Boyles' box on his way home. Mrs Boyle found it with her mail the following day.

She must have sat all afternoon in her kitchen, looking at the drawing, turning away, turning back, while pain and disbelief turned into rage. She ran into the street – a large woman, pretty once, with rounded parts softened by middle age – and met Gordon midway between our steps and her gate. He was alone, I ten steps behind with my classmate Lois Munro (out of custom, not friendship: she lived two houses down).

I have captioned it The Event in Orchard Street. (Once I used Terrible Event but it's too stark for adjectives.) Mrs Boyle burst from her gate. She seized Gordon and shook him, and when his shirt tore and part of the sleeve came away in her hand, struck him on the face with it like a whip – Gordon squealing. She forced him on to his knees in the gravel, dragged him up, shook him again, rattled him, all the time crying, 'Cruel boy, wicked boy.' Gordon's schoolbag bucked on his back. His cowlick bounced on his forehead and his shocked eyes – where was he? – found only bits of her, a leg, a face. I ran around them, looking for a way to save my brother. I caught a handful of Mrs Boyle's dress and swung on it, which made her grip him two-handed. The piece of paper she had screwed into his face as she attacked fell under her feet. I swung on her, skidding in the gravel as she freed one hand and slapped him – ringing slaps on his brow and cheeks. My best help was screaming, which brought Mrs Dandridge from her house and Mother tumbling down our steps – she skinned her palms and knees – and the Brotts' mongrel dog leaping over its fence. It ran nipping ankles round Gordon and Mrs Boyle until Mrs Dandridge kicked it away. She unlocked Mrs Boyle, and the woman collapsed; rage and strength went out of her, she deflated like a bladder, while Mother seized Gordon, putting blood-marks on him, and hurried him out of danger up our steps.

Lois Munro had run as far as her gate. Mrs Dandridge took Mrs Boyle into her house. The yellow dog cornered the sheet of paper against our milk-box. I shooed him off and ran with it up our path. The paper was the key. I stopped, panting, at our back door, uncrumpled it, looked at Gordon's drawing, and knew that we, the Ferrys, were out of step. It was gone in a flash – Gordon's sobbing in the kitchen, Mother's crying, were too much. I ran in and joined myself to them. Only later, when Gordon's face was washed and Mother had painted iodine on her hands and sponged her knees and Gordon had been placed, heaving sobs, on his bed, and Father was home, only then – three Ferrys – did we smooth the paper on the kitchen table and look at what he had drawn.

The desert sand was made with pencil dots. Mike Boyle flung up his arms and died, with his rifle spilling in the air. 'Private Boyle' stood in capitals at the head. 'He died for King and Country,' Gordon printed. 'Do not grieve.' (He was top of his class in spelling.)

'Well meant' became our saving phrase. Father used it to Mr Boyle when he walked across with the priest to talk to us that night. Mr Boyle agreed. He added that he knew Gordon was not a bad boy. 'Thoughtless,' Father Colvin supplied. I think he was there to see that Mr Boyle did not lose his calm and shout or cry. I was fascinated by his back-to-front collar and black suit. He was not like ordinary men but came from the world of dead soldiers and grief, and I felt our kitchen was not good enough, was somehow mean, while Mr Boyle, with his rough hands and working-man's face, was good enough. I felt as I had with Gordon's drawing – out of step. (Our kitchen was not mean, of course. We had coloured linoleum and papered walls and a table with turned legs and the first electric stove in the street, and Father's BSc degree stood framed on the mantelpiece.)

'Can we speak to the boy?' Father Colvin said.

'No,' Mother said.

'He's sleeping. He's had a nasty shock,' Father said.

'Attacked like that,' Mother said. 'If Mrs Boyle had bothered to see me . . .'

'It was well meant. You must see that,' Father said.

'And calling him wicked,' Mother said.

'My boy is dead,' Mr Boyle said.

'Come on, Michael, let's go home,' Father Colvin said.

'Lily's had too much to bear. She'll never get over it,' Mr Boyle said.

'We're sorry,' Father said. 'Gordon meant well. It was misjudged.'

None of us went further than that, although I knew, I *knew*, we were out of step. Father showed Mr Boyle and Father Colvin out the door. He put his hand on Mr Boyle's shoulder – 'Mick, I'm sorry.' He meant for everything and all of us. Mr Boyle lifted his shoulder, not rudely but in a rejecting way.

When the door was closed and the footsteps gone we went into Gordon's bedroom. He had heard the men walking up the path and crawled under his bed and not crawled out as he heard them go. The empty room made Mother scream but Father, instantaneous in knowing, went down on his knees: 'Come on, son. Come out.' He put his arm into the dark, took Gordon's arm and pulled him – gently, gently – out. Gordon was curled up like a lobster and red with crying. Father stood him up, straightened him, took out his handkerchief and wiped his nose. He held Gordon in his arms and let him cry.

'I thought they'd like it,' Gordon wailed.

'You meant well,' Father said.

'I wanted . . . I wanted . . .'

'We have to be careful of what other people feel,' Father said.

We got over it, and quickly too. No more Boyle boys were killed. And Mother still ran across the road if it rained when Mrs Boyle was out, unpegged her washing and put it in the basket in her wash-house. But the feeling in Orchard Street was against us. I felt it in cooler smiles and offers of kindness rebuffed: 'Can I help carry your groceries, Mrs Dandridge?' 'No thank you, Alice. I can manage.'

'Out of step' came less frequently into my mind. 'Different' more often. 'Better' too. Father was a chemist and had his own shop. He didn't work on the railways or catch the train each morning to a factory in Auckland. He smoked tailor-made cigarettes, not roll-your-owns. He made compost, scientifically, and dug it into our garden, turning the yellow clay into 'good rich soil'. All sorts of things. He had two shelves of books – history and science and several poetry books – and although Mother didn't read, even magazines, even the paper, she knew things 'the way women know' and was more sensitive than most, Father said. And Gordon was top of his class. I was top too.

When I write that we were better I don't mean we were snobs. I mean that we were in the wrong place and also – it stretches understanding – the wrong time. It was the 1940s. The war was on. When I look at us I see 1920s people. It was possible to be apart in that earlier time, show cleverness and learning and refinement, without causing resentment or ridicule. So I understand. 'The war effort' and 'pulling together' and later on 'getting the country back on its feet' blurred all sorts of distinctions in the 40s.

But although we, the Ferrys, were in a way lost, we bounced like rubber balls on the ground of Father. He moved with certainty and lightness, as though making dance steps on a sprung floor like that one in the hall Gordon took me to on one of my visits to Wellington: the Majestic Cabaret – it's not there now. In appearance Father was like the priest, Father Colvin: both of them big men with white faces and black hair. Father never tanned in the sun. When he mowed the lawns or worked in the garden he wore a straw hat and a long-sleeved shirt. He never wore shorts. Exercise turned his face bright red, as though with some huge embarrassment. He sat in the shade cooling off as Mother brought him lemonade or a glass of beer. Gradually, over an hour or two, his face returned to its milky white. I pictured a contest inside him – the chemicals for heat fizzing angrily while the ones for coolness worked in a patient way, returning him to 98.6 degrees Fahrenheit, where he could be comfortable.

It was not that Father wasn't a physical man. He and Mother played tennis before the war. They were mixed doubles champions at the Holy Cross Club on the other side of the macrocarpa hedge behind our house. 'We're not holy and we don't cross ourselves,' Father said, 'but your mother's good-looking so they let us in.' He was second on the men's singles ladder. Earlier he played rugby for the Loomis team. In a photo I've just fetched from the shoebox in my wardrobe he wears a striped jersey with the collar turned up and holds a ball under his arm. What a handsome young man. What a natural smile. But he doesn't look as if he's ready to run and pass and tackle. There's a leaning more to moderate solutions, to sorting things out with an easy word. Others would not see it in the photo. They need my eye. Father, young Earl Ferry, is ready to lead in benevolence and humility. He's ready to show how we need each other, how everyone is special although no one must stand out.

Where does it come from? His own father was a dour small-town chemist, a widower at forty, a lawn bowler, wanting no more than to roll weighted balls on the shaved grass and hear them click. Their kissing was the closeness he required; he needed no family intimacies. In human feeling Father had made a standing start. No line of continuity seemed to exist between the old man rolling balls on the unnatural lawn and the younger one, white-jacketed in his shop (our shop), smoothing Gordon's cowlick, retying my bow, then thieving cough drops for us from the jar on the counter – he hummed a tune, looking at the ceiling – and sending us home with a kiss for Mother.

We spied on Grandfather after school. We peeped on tiptoe over the square-topped hedge enclosing the Loomis Bowling Club. There was something forbidden about him, and a mystery in how the bowls slowed down but kept on rolling. They leaned at the cringing jack and took possession of it. When Grandfather turned his eyes in our direction we ducked out of sight and knelt on the gravel path, trying not to breathe.

We had him once a year, for Christmas dinner. He and Father talked about the shop. It was easy to see he had no interest. We saw him animated only once: the town council had proposed digging up the bowling club greens and planting vegetables for the war effort. 'I'll shoot any bastard who comes through the gate with a spade,' Grandfather said.

'Language, please,' Mother said.

He leaned on her space like a weighted ball. 'You've overcooked this mutton. I like mine with a bit of blood in it.'

Father had done his apprenticeship in Grandfather's shop. Later he completed a Bachelor's degree in chemistry but came back to Ferry's the Chemist in the Loomis main street after working several years for a drug company. In 1940 he bought out Grandfather. He learned how to handle the old man by stepping back emotionally and refusing to be hurt by sarcasm and abuse. 'Take it easy, Dad,' he said in a voice weighted gently with understanding – used those words at the table on Christmas day before Mother could defend her cooking. Grandfather answered with an impatient grunt and stumped away as soon as pudding was over.

'Poor old chap. It's no fun living alone,' Father said.

He sent Gordon and me around to Grandfather's house with the presents he had left behind: hankies and socks and pipe tobacco.

'Leave them on the table,' Grandfather said. He was listening to band music on his gramophone.

I goose-stepped back down his path with my arms rigid at my sides. 'Don't,' Gordon whispered, 'he might see.'

Someone might hear, someone might see: two fears of his childhood. Yet he was not nervous or cringing, but sensitive. It's a state almost guaranteeing unpopularity. Gordon avoided the danger by running fast. He ran, Father said, like a hare, and won the sprint races at the Loomis School sports and later at the Western Suburbs sports. The rugby coach put him on the wing, where he scooted around opposing players on his way to the try line. I never saw Gordon in those fights for the ball where feet and elbows flail and gouging gets done and people are left bleeding on the ground. They threw 'the pill' out wide to him and away he went. He did not have, the coach said, a football brain, and never knew exactly what he was meant to do but hesitated a moment after catching the ball. But when he had worked out where he was meant to go – sometimes his team-mates had to point – he took off. 'Go, Gordy,' the cry rang out. How lucky he was not to be punched and hair-pulled like the fat boy.

Someone might see, and not be angry or vengeful but offended. Be hurt. That was his fear. It was Father's lesson grafted on to him and flourishing. Concern plumped his organs. Pity sweated from his pores.

Now I'm being vengeful and I order myself to turn about – to understand. Well, I do. I've put down that stuff about the Boyles, and I say one more time 'well meant'. Yet Gordon had ways of serving himself. I tot them up and the sum is as openended as disappointment; but when I draw back to see the days passing, see him grow tall, hear his voice break, there's just one: he served himself by feeling good about serving other people. I have proof of it but the time's not now.

If I step forward, it's only as a way of stepping him back.

I've spent the last few minutes holding hands, my two hands equal, left in right, right in left, with the thumbs crossed over. It's a way of feeling human warmth. And a way of admitting that I lied above. I don't hold Gordon in reserve. I put myself ahead of him out of interest.

I am Alice Ferry. I have not always held hands with myself – although there's nothing wrong with it, let me say. It gives better warmth than the friendships I retain, and intimate satisfactions and knowledge, deep knowledge, that cannot be shared. I've never been lonely, although I've wept and shivered a few times at being alone. It's a way of finding myself.

I'm an ordinary woman, with that ordinariness, a kind of homeliness, that becomes desirable when you recognise it. I've done good work and been honoured for it. My gifts have always pleased me but not lifted me above myself. What gifts are those? Intelligence, energy, persistence, intuition. More than enough for my two-stranded professional life.

Father had been apprenticed to his father and I became apprenticed to mine. The shop was opposite the Loomis railway yards, between Hudson the Butcher and the billiard saloon, where the local boys swaggered in with fags in their mouths. None of them interested me. I could look up from serving at the counter – liniments, mouthwashes, suppositories – and watch steam engines take on water from the tall red-painted tank over the road from our door. The stoker hauled the pipe on its cord, flipped back the boiler lid, inserted the limp leather and it swelled to rigidity. The memory excites me even now. (I'm not silly, I know why.) Beyond the triple railtracks the blacksmith beat red-hot iron plates in his forge. These were men. The boys on the footpath, raucous for my attention, pimpled (poor things), hands deep in pockets, round-shouldered from choice, were foetus-like, not properly in the world. They had a narrow passage to force through and years to live before they could stand on the engine like the stoker or hammer iron glowing from the forge. I leaned sideways to watch those proper men, then stood upright to serve our customers. Q-tol. Dr Scholl's Foot Cream. And you say she's teething, poor wee thing. Steedman's Powders are the best for that.

Why did those boys gather in front of our shop and boast in shouting voices about potting the black? They were worse than a sawmill and made our customers flinch, until Father angled his head from the dispensary: 'Go out and send them away. But be polite, Alice.'

'I'll call the police,' I told them.

'It's just old Banksie,' they said. 'He's scared to go in. He wants some frenchies for tonight.'

'I don't, Alice. They're lying,' Banksie cried, flushing red up to the line of his Brylcreemed hair.

'I'm phoning them.'

'Alice, I don't. I don't want those.'

Inside, I picked up the phone and they dispersed. They wanted me. I stood white-smocked in the cool shop like a lily in a garden nook. They wanted to pluck me, despoil me, and one or two love me perhaps. Was it my contempt that drew them, or my blue eyes and red lips and yellow hair?

I was not saving myself for Mr Right. Nothing as silly as that. I simply enjoyed my coolness, my interests, my work and the contents of my mind. I had a sufficiency of good things and no curiosities of the flesh those unfinished boys could satisfy.

I was in the *Pharmaceutical Journal's* February list, 1949: *Successful Students. Section C. Biographical Notes. Miss A. M. Ferry:* Is nineteen years of age. She attended Epsom Girls' Grammar School, Auckland, passing matriculation in 1945 and gaining her Higher Leaving Certificate the following year. She was keen on debating and was in the school tennis and hockey teams. Miss Ferry enjoys camping and the open-air life and has climbed to the top of Mt Ngauruhoe. She was apprenticed to her father, E. J. Ferry of Loomis, in 1947 and passed 'B' the same year. She hopes to begin a BSc degree this year. Miss Ferry is interested in the study of native flora.

It seemed more ladylike to say flora than fungi. I did not wish to be thought unfeminine or odd. Hockey, climbing mountains, the open-air life sounded thick-ankled and hairy-legged. Nor did I wish to share. Fungi remained my secret, although Father and Mother knew, and Gordon of course.

It began with prettiness and sweetness: violets spreading under our hedge. I lay with my face in them, drinking in the scent. I picked posies for Mother and carried bunches tied with ribbon to my teacher at school. Honeysuckle spilled down the bank by the creek. I climbed into it and lay as though on a sofa, nipping flower stems between my finger and thumbnail, taking sips of nectar fit for a bee.

I became flower monitor in Standard Four. Mother taught me arranging from a little book she found on a bring-and-buy stall. We planted pansies by the back door and rows of marigolds and Livingstone daisies by the path. Bedding in seedlings and poking bulbs into the soil turned me away from the girliness of colour and scent, from 'ooh' and 'aah' and 'heavenly' and the fussiness of arranging. I discovered growth. I don't mean by revelation, I mean interest. I saw what happened next, and how, and why.

Science is knowing. Completion as much as anything attracts me. I don't place this weight on the shoulders of a child. I did not know what I was getting into but absorbed through my eyes and fingertips and kept each new thing in a memory box. Each was as natural as freckles on my wrists or hairs on my head.

I've been meticulous in my scientific life. I'm close and steady in picking up and putting down, in looking and acquiring, but sometimes I almost faint with joy in reaching the end. I'm delirious with completion but remain milky-faced, uninflected, and don't celebrate until I'm alone: a glass of wine, a cigarette, Tchaikovsky at full bore on the record player, and later on a pizza ordered in and a tot of whisky before bed. I can be sure of sleeping well.

But I'm getting ahead. When did the mycologist begin her growth in the child?

It's hard to say. Mushrooms in the paddocks? Toadstools under the pines? The brown smoke of spores from a puffball trodden on? I don't think so. Blight on potato leaves? That was a fungus too. *Perenospora infestens*, Father said. His degree was in chemistry but he had studied botany as well. He told me other names. The mushrooms were a family, *Agaricus campestris*. Toadstools were

Agarics too. But although naming pleased me – and the difference between genus and species, which he explained, and the deadly danger of eating the wrong thing – it was the idea of growing in secret places, in the dark, that attracted me. Unlike flowers, fungi did not open to the sun. They were, Father said, parasites. They did not live by photosynthesis, which he claimed (wrongly) was more natural, but by breaking down other living things, making them decay and feeding on the dead. He meant to make me shiver. Instead he turned me into a mycologist.

It sounds unhealthy. But no, it was a stepping out. It was passing through a narrow door into an ill-lit room and finding a worm-eaten chest in the corner, opening it and finding diamonds, emeralds, gold dubloons, crowns inlaid with rubies and amethysts, and a suit of armour made to ward off each sword blow and lance thrust. Why shouldn't I be lyrical about the study that has filled my life? Fungi are my treasure. Fungi are my burden of work. I've battled throughout my career, taken blows, returned them, but always been armoured in the knowledge: this is mine, this is what I do. And now, retired, I walk in my garden among the flowers, slide my eye down the fall of oak and pine and native to the sea, and enjoy it all, enjoy the beauty of chlorophyll and photosynthesis, while whispering to my secret workers busy in the dark: I know you're there.

There are jokes I'll not repeat about women mycologists. I've put up with smirks and sneers, and at other times hidden my primary trade behind my secondary, limnology. Lakes and creeks sound healthy. You can even tack on swamps without making the ignorant and prejudiced step away as though you smell bad. But, essentially, I could not be touched. Whether working with smut or rust in a Petri dish or collecting green algae in waterways, I was armoured in, not enthusiasm or belief, but interest. It's a necessary condition.

You can glow, you can sparkle with interest, while keeping your attention firm and your countenance still.

I was not understood. I was not liked. It does not matter.

Back to the chemist shop.

Passing 'B' and 'C' gave me no trouble, although the examiners complained that the overall standard was poor, especially in practical work. Oral and written pharmacy were no problem. I wrote a five-page essay on the sulphonamides, where apparently most candidates wrote five or six lines of vague therapeutics. But in practical dispensing I really excelled. We were asked to prepare calcium bromide, which requires a calculation to neutralise the hydrobromic acid, but oh, the thick deposits most of the other candidates were left with in their bottles! It bewildered me. How could they get such an easy thing wrong? And neutralising Spts Aeth. Nit. – it's not a set amount, it depends on the sample. I complained to Father that these people might soon be dispensing. Some of them did not even know how to sterilise a procaine solution. They were helpless without an autoclave. And as I complained I began to boast, began to like myself very well.

Father said, 'They haven't had the advantage of someone really teaching them.' He was not praising himself but gently deflating me and turning my eyes outwards to other people. I would not look at them except to pour scorn. It was my first significant rebellion. I wanted my achievements seen, I wanted them praised. I was not going to spend my life as a small-town chemist like Father. He saw the thought move across my eyes, and gave a little smile and a nod.

'I'm pleased you've done so well, Alice. I'll phone your mother, shall I? We'll have a special dinner tonight.'

Oyster soup, lamb chops, a date roll for pudding? My cleverness, my brilliance, deserved more. Gordon read my concealed pout (our knowing of each other had ease and quickness and intensity): 'We should go to the pictures, eh? There's a good one at the Delta.'

Mother and Father agreed, so we drove to New Lynn, where the film was *Quartet*, four Somerset Maugham stories. I found two of them silly but the one about the woman poet whose husband fails to understand her made me wipe my eye; and the other, called, I think, 'The Alien Corn', wove its situation into mine and left me soft with pity, melting with it, and shrill with the horror of anticipated failure, and hard with determination, which won out. A young man (Dirk Bogarde, I remember), ambitious to be a concert performer, persuades a famous pianist to hear him play. She listens and says, 'No, you are an amateur. Your playing is square.' Relief from the young man's girlfriend and parents, who want him to be a country gentleman. The woman pianist, invited, takes off her rings and plays. The difference between amateur and professional is clear. Even I, unmusical, can hear it. The young man hears. The moment is dreadful as he understands. But there is room only for the truth. His parents thank the pianist and she leaves. They sigh and smile, preparing for the future. The young man says he's getting ready too – for shooting pheasants, or is it grouse? How could they not have understood? A gunshot sounds . . .

Anything even roughly parallel would have done. This seemed exact. I would not follow my grandfather and father. I would not spend my days in the dispensary, with gargles and mouthwashes and kidney mixture, or chat at the counter, selling friar's balsam, lint and cottonwool, or, with a little nod and averted eyes, slip one of those brown-paper packets from under the counter – Durex or Wife's Friend pessaries. The pianist took off her heavy rings and put her naked hands on the keys. She was no longer foreign – Hungarian, was she, Russian? – but suddenly herself, and all the others – the mother and father, the girlfriend, the young man too –

were pushed back to the perimeter of her life. I overlooked that my family placed no pressure on me, that their hopes were only for my happiness. I needed to be resentful. I was breaking out from Father's way of widening his gaze to everyone.

I cared no more that Dirk Bogarde had shot himself. 'I'm never going to wear rings on my hands,' I declared. I've kept to that.

'I think it was an accident,' Mother said.

'Yes,' Father said. 'I don't think he knew there was a bullet in the gun.'

'I'm going to take botany,' I said.

I meant that I would be a mycologist. Meanwhile, what would Gordon be?

'There's no need to choose yet. Take your time,' Father said.

It was already plain he would not be a chemist. At primary school he had come top in every subject, but something derailed him at secondary. He became disconnected from the practical. Nor could he take on board abstractions. I suppose it had to do with puberty, with things already fixed in him – gentility, notions of purity – uniting to divorce him from the new part of himself that made itself known. He was in turmoil, and, to use the cant phrase, in denial. I've never been troubled in that way, so I'm in the dark. All he has ever told me was that it took ten years to get himself right, which meant, I think, to understand that sex was not some secret dirty thing but natural, and to get on better terms with his natural self.

He could not take the step to algebra and geometry. He could not understand chemistry. I tried coaching him but his brain refused to function with planes, angles, symbols, formulae, with elements and compounds, even when they changed colour and smoked and smelled. The only reactions his mind could fasten on were human ones, and it's no surprise that in English he still came top.

Families are factories for neurosis. But I won't speculate about Gordon. I'll remember. Our days are multitudinous. If I turn aside from unhappy things, it's not through fear or cowardice but out of love. There's a superstition involved: even now I can do him good.

He still ran fast and still played football. I went along to see him play for his school first fifteen. The match took place on the Auckland Grammar School grounds above the prison, where as I stood on the sideline and watched Gordon's team go down to defeat I imagined I could hear prisoners breaking rocks in the quarry. The game bored me. There was lots of struggling in the mud and Gordon kept out of it. The big fat-muscled boys who competed for the ball reminded me of pigs nose down at a trough. Steam rose off them and the smell of their sweat invaded the sidelines. Late in the game the ball squirted out from a scrum and stopped at Gordon's feet. By this time he knew what to do. 'Go, Gordy.' He made thirty or forty yards before an Auckland Grammar player came at him from the side. Gordon tried to fend him off, but his opponent caught him around the knees and lifted him. Gordon hung in the air for a moment, then his stiffened arm speared at the ground as though trying to drive itself in. I saw it shorten as the joint popped out. The shock sprang between us like electricity and propelled me forwards, one step, two, until my leaden good sense returned.

The coach helped him away as the game continued. 'My sister?' Gordon said, looking around. I approached coolly and placed my white fingertips on his unnatural elbow. 'I don't think it's broken, just dislocated,' Gordon said. I was surprised to see him red-faced not white, and almost merry, but knew him well enough to understand that dislocating an elbow was an achievement. 'Bad luck, eh? This is my sister, Mr Seed.'

Mr Seed. A sad-looking, clumsy-mannered fellow. Big-boned, soft-faced – attracting hyphenated adjectives – slow-spoken, but decisive in his way. 'I'm taking him to the hospital. Would you like to come?'

I thanked him. 'Don't faint, Gordon.' The red was fading from his face as shock set in. I helped him into the back seat of Mr Seed's car. He half reclined, preventing me from getting in beside him. The zambuck had strapped his arm above and below the elbow. I saw how bad the dislocation was, shortening his arm by several inches and pressing white bulbs of bone against the skin. A painful injury but Gordon seemed to think the event a happy one, for he still grinned.

'I'm sorry to be such a nuisance, Sir.'

'Don't be stupid, Ferry,' Mr Seed said. He settled in the driver's seat, more aware of me than of Gordon – put off balance by the pretty sister. He apologised for the broken spring in the car seat.

'I'm all right,' I said, fitting myself to one side of it, which allowed me to hold Gordon's hand. It was as damp as a boletus and as cold as the creek. 'I think we should get him there as fast as we can.'

'Right,' said Mr Seed. He was torn between discretion and me, which led to braking one moment and acceleration the next; but we reached the hospital safely and surrendered Gordon to a nurse. She took one look at his elbow and hurried him into a cubicle, where a doctor scarcely more than a boy himself examined him. The nurse fetched a trolley and they wheeled Gordon away down a corridor.

'It's a dangerous game. He needs to put on a bit more beef,' Mr Seed said.

We waited side by side on bony chairs. He told me about his own injuries: torn calf muscles, a dislocated finger that had allowed him for an hour to point around corners (he laughed), and a badly sprained ankle that had left his right foot colder than his left. He still suffered from that. For a moment I thought he was asking me to feel. I understood how badly Mr Seed wanted me. If I had not been worried about Gordon I might have played with him. I knew already that I liked older men, and Mr Seed had a puppyish maturity – I mean a hardening by experience without an understanding of what life was about – that might have entertained me for a while. But I'm speaking with a smarter voice than I possessed at nineteen, and will simply say, Seed's time wasn't right.

We talked about chemistry, which he taught. I told him about my interest in native flora, keeping fungi to myself. He hunted for openings until I asked him if he was married. What a blusher he was. He said yes. We talked naturally after that. He went off to telephone his wife and came back with an ice-cream for me. We waited more than two hours on our numbing chairs as more football injuries came in. The young victims seemed so pleased with themselves.

The nurse brought Gordon to us in a wheelchair. He was woozy from an anaesthetic. The dislocation had been so bad the doctor had needed an orderly to help him pull the joint into place, stretching Gordon's arm to its proper length. We wheeled him to Mr Seed's car and fitted him in. This time I sat beside him, holding him upright and keeping him warm. His arm was strapped tightly and held in a sling, and no, no, he repeated drunkenly, it didn't hurt. I called out in Avondale that he was going to be sick but Mr Seed could not stop in time. Gordon vomited between his feet. 'Sorry. Sorry,' he mumbled. I wiped his mouth and did not apologise. The stupid Seed had put Gordon in the game so he must put up with the consequences.

We had meant to go to the pictures in town after the game, so Mother and Father were not alarmed by our lateness. But Mother screamed when she saw Mr Seed helping Gordon up the path – her dying-fall, I-knew-it-was-going-to-happen scream, like a seabird.

Gordon tried to break away into the wash-house. 'Got to wash his car,' he mumbled.

'Go inside, Gordon,' I ordered. 'I'll do it.'

While Mother put him on his bed and sponged off his football mud and Father heard about the injury from Mr Seed, I scraped Gordon's vomit on to a hearth shovel and washed the wet car floor with Lysol on a rag. There, I thought, I've disinfected myself from Mr Seed; but that was unfair. It was life that infected me, and curiosity and self-recognition, making me ready for the parts I had to play. And Seed was a pleasant, inconsequential man who tried his best to help Gordon – and impress himself on me. Didn't work, but I bear him no grudge. He went on to be principal of one of the new secondary schools that sprang up around Auckland in the 60s.

And I went on, and Gordon went on . . .

That's too fast.

He dislocated his elbow playing football. I've suggested it was a happy event. His self emerged and caused him no bother on that day. Not that he knew it in those terms. But his little pause for thought before action was gone. As well as that, he was a hero – that's what New Zealand men become when they break their bones in their barbarous game.

Gordon's elbow stayed too weak for him to play again. He took up tennis to strengthen it and did quite well, although reluctance overcame him when he found himself in a winning position. He should have been club champion at the Loomis Lawn Tennis Club but gave the game away each time to someone wanting it more.

Father and I agreed that I should work mornings in the shop and do my first two BSc units part-time. I travelled to Auckland by train at first, then changed to the bus, which put me down closer to the university. I saw how Loomis was moving its centre from around the station to the stretch of the Great North Road between the bridges, where the ABC buses came in. A man called Jock Imrie was putting up blocks of shops. The Bank of New Zealand had opened a branch and the Post Office had plans for a new building. It worried me that Father was left in the dying part of town, next door to the billiard rooms. Hudson the Butcher had shifted to the Great North Road.

'If you don't go, there'll be another chemist,' I said.

'I will, Alice. I will. I've already put a word in with Jock Imrie.'

He was not normally indecisive. It was Grandfather's sudden interest in the shop that delayed him. 'Ferry's' had been opposite the station since my great-grandfather had opened there in the 1890s. Grandfather wanted it to go on. He'd had a series of small strokes that finished him for bowls. When he tried to hold one of those heavy balls it tipped out of his hand. Coming into the shop was his new game. He sat on a chair in the dispensary and demanded to know what Father was mixing – how much of this, how much of that, and who it was for, and why weren't the old medicines good enough, and why should the government pay for prescriptions, why should his taxes go for bludgers who should be able to look after themselves? Father confessed to me that it 'wore him to a frazzle', but he refused to make Grandfather stay away. He meant, I think, to keep on in the shop until the old man's interest declined.

'He'll live till he's ninety,' I said.

Father told me not to be cruel. 'I sometimes don't like the way you seem to be going, Alice.'

I can't remember any other time he was so direct.

I told Grandfather one day that the shop should shift. He stamped his walking-stick on the floor. 'This is where Loomis is. Right here. Jock Imrie can keep his Great North Road. Those shops of his look like a row of dunnies.'

Father calmed him, worried that his anger would cause another stroke. He drove him home, and Mother went round to make him lunch. Gordon dropped in when he got off the school train, and Father paid a visit each night to see Grandfather into bed. The old bugger – yes, bugger – never spoke a word of thanks.

'What do you talk about with him?' I asked Gordon.

'I don't. I put on records. The Black Dyke Mills Band. He really loves those things. I like them too. And his comedy records. Do you know, he can laugh? I take one off and he just says, "Next."'

Grandfather had a stack of records by Scotch and English comedians: sketches, songs, monologues by Max Miller and Stanley Holloway, and Flanagan and Allen. Gordon wound up the old gramophone and put them on, starting always with Grandfather's favourite – I forget the name and the players, but a man asks his friend how he should propose to the girl he loves, Nausea Bagwash. He must go down on one knee, the friend advises, and say, 'I have come to press my suit.' The lover is not very bright. 'Nausea,' he cries, 'I have come to iron my trousers.'

'It makes him laugh every time,' Gordon said. 'But I guess "Brahn Boots" is the one he really likes' – a sentimental monologue about a man who turns up to his mother's funeral wearing brown boots. 'We didn' know, 'e didn' say, 'e'd give 'is uvver boots awa-ay. But, brahn boots!'

'It makes him cry,' Gordon said.

'Pull the other one,' I said. Old men had worn-out eyes always leaking moisture. I wished another stroke on Grandfather, his terminal one. I did not see why we should be *serving* him while he gave nothing back.

Mother sometimes sent me round to his place on Saturdays when she wanted a rest from making his lunch and putting his dinner ready in the oven. He did not ask for records when I was there. He sat in his armchair in the living-room, which smelled of rotting window frames and mutton fat and him, with the bar heater baking his leather soles, and called me from the kitchen to fill his teacup, pick up the *Herald*, which he'd dropped out of reach, scratch his back – 'No, lower down' – where there was an itch, shift the table closer with his medicine, pull the curtain over to block the sun . . . I was no sooner out of the room than he called me back: 'Alice.' What a bark it was, what a snake-hiss at the end.

'You can do that yourself, you're not helpless,' I said.

The smell of his slippers cooking overpowered the other smells. I warned him they'd catch fire. Then I did not bother, although one of my tasks was to shift the heater back or forward as Grandfather overheated or grew cold. I knew what he was up to, watching me bend, watching me stretch (to free the curtain on the runner or straighten a picture on the wall), getting looks up my skirt and down my blouse.

'You've grown to be a big girl, Alice,' he said.

'I bet you've got some boyfriends,' he said.

He had a dozen of these remarks, leading up to me smoothing his lap-rug. A generous granddaughter might have obliged. I don't have an ounce of generosity of that sort.

I lay awake at night, thinking how easy it would be to pinch some pentobarbitone and falsify the dangerous drugs book. A teaspoon in his mashed potatoes . . . But the worst I ever did was tip Grandfather's lamb's fry and bacon in his lap and leave him to clean up the mess: 'And don't complain to Mother or I'll tell her what you do.'

He must have said something because Mother never sent me back. I wonder if he had tried the same sort of thing with her. The look that passed between us when he died contained not sorrow but relief.

31

Father found him half in, half out of his chair. His trouser leg was scorching and ready to combust. Another two or three minutes would have done it. Fire would have been a cleaner death than he deserved. But he lay unconscious in hospital for several days. 'He's very deep down,' the doctor said. 'Speak to him. You can never tell what people hear.'

I had nothing to say.

'You can hold his hand,' the nurse said.

I left that to Father and Gordon. They murmured at him and breathed on him. 'We want you to come back, Dad. Don't go,' Father said. He smoothed Grandfather's hair and massaged his big flat hand that had caressed only bowling balls. Gordon leaned and whispered: 'Grandpa. Stanley Holloway.'

'He can't hear,' I said.

'Brahn boots,' Gordon whispered.

'Oh, for God's sake,' I said.

'I can make him smile. You watch.' He lowered his head and breathed in Grandfather's gristly ear: 'Nausea, I have come to iron my trousers.' He smiled at me as though from the bottom of a pool. 'See?' he breathed.

'He did not.'

'Yes, he did. Watch.' He repeated the stupid line; and there might have been the jumping of a nerve in Grandfather's cheek. I did not stay to argue; left Gordon reciting there. I could not believe Grandfather might come back to life. It would be as horrible as a squashed beetle twitching its legs. Yet it would not have seemed strange to me if Gordon had worked a miracle. He functioned differently – he turned away (a natural turning) from common feelings into uncommon, where doors might open and good be done. He did not mind seeming ridiculous. I had no idea what he would bring Grandfather back for . . . but enough of this.

He died that night. Mother and I exchanged our smile. Father was sad but somehow completed. And Gordon sighed as though pleased by a scene in a movie.

I thought, There'll be some money from the house. I supposed Father would get it but felt some should come to me for my stretching and bending. Father said we should choose something to remember the old man by. 'No thanks,' I said. Gordon took half a dozen records but I don't recall him ever playing them.

The house went to Grandfather's sister in Blenheim. So the old man drove his last bowl and knocked us out of the head.

'Ah well, he must have had his reasons,' Father said.

TWO

Mrs Imrie was comfortable in her figure but unsatisfied in her life. She came into the shop for lipstick, rouge, face powder, bottles of scent; for Micapon for her migraines and Dr Scholl's Foot Cream for her feet, which she told me her husband had to massage every night or she'd lie awake with shooting pains in her toes like a shoemaker elf hammering tacks.

'Look after your feet, dear. That's the voice of experience.'

She painted and powdered heavily, which I thought a waste with her good skin. She said I could do things with my appearance if I tried, I could be a cover girl; and she picked out lipsticks that suited my colouring and tried to make me put them on in the shop.

'No, I can't, Mrs Imrie. I'm allergic. I'll get a rash.'

'And look at your hair. I could really do things with that, it's so fine.'

Jock Imrie had found her when he called for his first wife at a beauty parlour in Auckland. The perm wasn't finished, so he observed able-bodied Josephine at his leisure as she moved about his wife with her implements. I imagined Mrs Imrie number one watching Jock's lust take shape in the mirror and a tear rolling down her cheek. Perhaps, though, she was relieved to be quit of him. He was a weaselly man who pointed at things he wanted with his nose.

Mrs Imrie – Josephine – confided in me: 'He's so busy at it. Every night.' She bought her Wife's Friend pessaries from our shop, asking for me at first, but later on not minding Father.

Josephine moved in with Jock Imrie soon after his wife left, and, wonder of wonders, it was the wife who got sued for adultery. Jock and Josephine married and went off straight away on a world trip, and it was that, I think, the trip, that persuaded Loomis to accept wife number two as respectable. We had loved the scandal, lapped it up, but the judgement we made on Jock was of a tut-tutting kind. He lived in a big two-storeyed house on three acres of ground sloping down to the creek. He drove a Jaguar car and owned racehorses. He was rich. It was no wonder women went after him.

His money came from Western Freight and Haulage, a company he started before the war. He owned twenty trucks when he sold out. Some people said he was a black marketeer. He dealt in war surplus for some years, there was no secret about that, but his lasting interest was in buying land and putting up buildings for sale or rent. It's interesting how words get degraded. 'Vision' has come to mean seeing opportunities to make money. Jock Imrie had vision. He saw where Loomis had to go and went there one step ahead. His first block of shops looked like cow sheds. After that he grew sophisticated. His name was raised in plaster above the veranda of his second block: Imrie's Buildings. The shop I wanted for Father was close to the intersection of Station Road and the Great North Road. A sporting goods store was opening on one side and a menswear shop on the other.

'We can get away from billiards and meat,' I said.

'Will you take some Micapon to Mrs Imrie?' Father said. 'Take the car.'

She used us in this way, even for eyebrow pencil and mascara, which I put on her doorstep, then rang the bell and left. I told Father she had a cheek; we should charge her for deliveries. A migraine was different. I rang the bell and waited, admiring the lawns and flowerbeds and trimmed hedges. It would be nice to have money, to have a big house and ornamental ponds and a scoria driveway and a gardener mopping his face on the hill at the back.

'Oh,' said Mrs Imrie, when she opened the door.

'I've brought your Micapon,' I said.

'I was hoping your father . . . It's getting bad, you see. I was going to ask about a double dose.'

'It tells you on the packet,' I said.

'Come in. Please. Please, dear. I need . . .'

If she wanted someone to talk to I thought she should pay. And I wondered about the migraine she was supposed to have. Her eyes seemed bright enough, her make-up was in place, and her brow was furrowed only with disappointment at finding me, not Father, at her door. I followed her into her sitting-room – her lounge.

'I was just lying on the sofa,' she said. 'Just keeping still. Will you pull the curtain across, dear? The light . . .'

She was wearing a silk housecoat and white fur mules and had cigarettes and magazines in reach. She kicked off the mules and lay down, then gave up her pretence and sighed.

'Jock's away. So maybe we could have a cup of tea.' The idea seemed to please her, remind her of life before Jock Imrie, for she said, 'The tea break at Marjorie's, I used to long for that. My swollen feet. And hair up my nose. And talk all the time, talk, talk, talk. It's always so quiet in your shop.'

'We get busy,' I said. 'We're busy now. So I'll have to go.'

'Just ten minutes. Five minutes? You've no idea how I miss good talks.'

I did not point out her contradiction. 'I can't stay long. I've got to do prescriptions before my bus.'

'Are you going somewhere?'

'To the university. I go every day.'

'What for? I thought the shop . . .'

'I'm doing botany.'

She could not grasp it. 'Plants?' she said.

'Yes. Trees. Flowers. Ferns. Algae. Moss' – although I had not got so far: no algae yet, no moss, and, to my disappointment, no fungi. 'Whatever grows.'

'Whatever for?'

'To find out about them. Work with them.' And I knew as I spoke that work was better, finding out was better than getting rich and lying on a sofa flicking through magazines all day.

'But doesn't it strain your eyes? Reading all those books you have to read? You don't want to wear glasses, Alice. Men don't like girls with red-rimmed eyes.'

'I don't care what men like,' I said.

'Oh, Alice.'

'I've got to go.'

Scoria crunched in the driveway, and silliness went out of her face. I saw how quick she was in things that had to do with men; saw lies chase across her face. Jock Imrie had come home when he wasn't expected.

'Ah, that's my husband,' she said, thinking easily after her quick jumping and busy-ness. 'I don't really want him now, so I'll just lie down. If you'll tell him about my migraine – will you do that?'

She stood up and her housecoat fell open, revealing frilly panties and a bra – and in that moment I knew. How quick my mind was, quicker than hers. I felt a forward-tilting in the part that under-stood, and took a little unwilled step at Mrs Imrie, which made her gasp. She pulled her housecoat tight and tied the belt, slipped on her mules.

'Help me, Alice,' she said, and ran away.

I went outside and found Jock Imrie standing by Father's car. The gardener, who must have been his spy, was walking away.

I said, 'Your wife's got a migraine. She's gone to bed.'

'Huh,' he said. He slapped Father's car to show how tinny it was.

'If you don't mind, I'd like to get in,' I said.

He stepped aside but not enough to give me room. His nose pointed at me and I thought, I could be the next Mrs Imrie.

'You're Earl Ferry's girl?'

'Yes.'

'Tell Earl I need to talk some business.'

'Now?'

'Yes, now. What's your name?'

'Alice.'

He pointed with his nose again. He did not want me for myself; I wasn't round enough, pneumatic enough. He wanted me to punish Father.

'I'm Jock Imrie.'

'I know. Do you mind getting out of my way?'

'You're a lippy one. Tell Earl–'

'I know what to tell him.'

I got in the car and drove away, not looking left or right or in the mirror to see what Jock Imrie would do. I went carefully through the gate and drove along beside the creek, out of his and Mrs Imrie's orbit. But after so much control I began to hyperventilate and gasp denials. I pulled at the wheel with weakened hands and managed to lift my foot off the accelerator on to the brake. The car stalled on the road shoulder. I climbed out and sat in the grass; stopped my mind; breathed deeply; got myself in hand. I'm able to do this. I'm not free from panicking, but can make myself hard and still – hands steady, face like a rock. Then I start up my mind again.

Father was, in his way, a sensualist. Good manners kept that part of his nature in control. Love, duty too, played a part: husband, father, son, dispenser of medicines, honest businessman, friendly neighbour, listener in adversity or grief. I could go on, but will end up trying too hard. I still believe him honest but know he was impure. I don't mean in succumbing to Mrs Imrie, but in using compassion in a sensual way. I won't say he fed on it, but there's no doubt it nourished him and made him fat. He pitied Mrs Imrie first and then he had her – which leaves out Mrs Imrie having him.

Sitting in the grass, I accepted Father. I gave him a bitter nod – hello. Then I came to the next part: what to do? Gordon would be better at this than me. But I was not going to let him hear a whisper of it. I made what I believed was a decision, although there was never more than one thing to do. When I had it fixed I stood up and brushed dust and grass seeds from my skirt, went half a dozen steps to the creek, looked at the squashy margin where I had learned to swim and at the deep green pool beyond, and thought, I'm out there now, I'm swimming alone. No Father and Mother drying me with a towel, both of them rubbing me and holding me tight, and holding each other too – a threesome. And now here's Gordon – a foursome. The memory flashed in colour, sharp-edged, but I turned away. Its usefulness was finished.

I drove to the shop, which was empty of customers, and went into the dispensary.

Father was making up prescriptions, and feigning an extra busy-ness. 'Ah,' he said, not looking up, 'I've done them, Alice. You can go for your bus.' He glanced up, smiled at me, then my coldness and stillness turned him pale.

'What is it?' he said.

'Mr Imrie wants to see you. He came home. But I wouldn't go yet. I think he's inside punching his wife.'

'Alice,' he said, and sat down heavily.

'Does Mother know what's happening?' I said.

'I don't know what you mean. Nothing's happening.'

'Don't tell lies, Father. Does she know?'

He closed his eyes. I saw hopes collapse in him as he found no way to go, no lie and no truth to tell; saw fear take hold.

'Does Mother know?' I said again.

'Nothing's happening. Nothing, Alice. It was only once. I couldn't help it. She . . . I can't tell you this.'

'I think you'd better. I'm grown up. I suppose she was in her housecoat. And panties and bra.'

The poor fishy opening of his mouth. His horror at me. 'I can't,' he began. He licked his lips, sent an upward glance at me, then lowered his eyes. 'She was crying. She was sad. He slaps her, Alice. He gets a kind of handful of her skin and twists –'

'Be quiet,' I said.

'So I tried –'

'Only once?'

'Yes. God's honour. I told her I couldn't any more.'

'But she thinks you can?'

'That's why I sent you there today instead of me. I'm not going back. I should never . . . I should have said . . .'

'Jock Imrie knows.'

'No. He can't . . .'

'He knows there's something. People like him always find out. He'll divorce her.'

'He won't, Alice. There's no proof.'

'He'll let some other chemist in his shops.'

'He won't. He promised me . . .'

'Was anything on paper?'

He opened his mouth, then closed it. Shook his head. Collapses, little subsidences, went on inside him. I was moved by pity, but not overwhelmed. I could not give the love and comfort he pleaded for, the daughter-strokings he must have felt were his right after his twenty years of loving me. The stitching between us was undone, and the most I could do was move a step towards him, touch his arm.

'Listen, Father. You've got to go round there and get a lease signed. Right now. You've got to find out what he knows. She might keep quiet. Did anyone see you when you were there?'

'I don't know.'

'Getting something signed, that's the main thing . . .'

I don't know why I went on with it. I knew we were – another use for that word – undone. Yet I sent him to Jock Imrie. I kept the little splintery hope of a miracle: that abjectness in Father would feed Imrie sufficiently to keep him quiet and allow him to be generous in the matter of the shop.

'Come on, Father.'

I helped him unbutton his lab coat. I took my place at the counter and served a customer as he drove away. Then I stood rigid with fear. In these situations didn't guns come out, or kitchen knives, pokers from the hearth come into play? I had said Jock Imrie would be punching his wife. When Father arrived he might use the shotgun he kept for hunting ducks. I had the absurd picture of Father putting up his hands like an actor in a western movie and Imrie pulling the trigger in spite of it. Yet I did not hang the closed sign on the door and jump on my bike and pedal round. I stood at the counter waiting for our next customer. Already, you see, I could judge men. Jock Imrie's revenge would last longer than a gunshot and cause no damage to himself. Letting Father have the shop might even be a way of stretching it out.

I missed my lectures that day. Father must have parked

somewhere and sat for an hour, shivering and weeping at the ruin of his life. He was red-eyed still when he arrived back at the shop. I hung the closed sign on the door and we went through the dispensary into the yard so no one would see us from the street. He sat down on an empty crate in an aged way, as though his shoulder joints were disconnected, and held his kneecaps to keep them from sliding off – and I stood over him, white-coated like an angel, although I meant neither to raise him nor condemn. I had grabbed his cigarettes from the bench as I passed and I tapped one out. He shook his head. I lit up – I started that day – and stood side on, with jutting hip and smoke curling from my palm.

'Well?' I said.

'It's no good, Alice.' His voice choked. He raised his hand to his face.

'What does that mean?'

'I didn't see her. Josie, I mean.'

'I'm not interested in any Josies. What did Mr Imrie say?'

'He came out . . .'

'Yes? Then what?'

'He told me I needn't bother getting out of my car. He said he knew I'd been . . . I can't use the language he used, Alice.'

'Isn't it the right word? Anyway, what next?'

'I told him I hadn't *been*. It was only once, and then it was only because he was hitting her. He said, "You should see her now," and I told him I'd call the police.'

'I imagine he only laughed at that.'

'Yes.' Father looked up, taking in the change in me. 'Alice, you shouldn't hear all this.'

'It's my business,' I said.

'He told me that he'd come home to catch us doing it. Him and

Ken Doole who works in the garden. He was going to get us for . . .'
Father could not say the word.

'Adultery,' I said.

He nodded. No more looking up. (In fact, now that I think of it, Father never met my eye again.) Some pity crept into me. I softened my edges.

'But he didn't find you.'

'He said it didn't matter because he was booting her out anyway. He said she'll be gone by tonight.'

'What about you?'

'He said he'll leave me stewing in my own juice for a while. Then he said . . .'

'The shop?'

Father nodded miserably. 'I asked him, and he laughed and said forget it. He said he's already got a chemist going in.'

So we were done for. I wanted to kick Father, but dropped the cigarette I had puffed at only twice and ground it under my shoe. Then I patted him, using the pity that slopped back into me – half a mugful. He seized my hand and kneaded it: 'Alice, Alice.'

'We'll have to work out what to do about it later on.'

'Yes. There'll be something. I've got all my customers. I've got my goodwill.'

'What you've got to do now is go home and tell Mother.'

His face turned up at me, white as a dinner plate, holed with the black hole of his mouth.

'No. She doesn't need –'

'Yes she does. And straight away. Before Jock Imrie lets her know.'

'He won't do that . . .'

'You don't think he's finished with you yet? You fucked his wife.'

'Alice . . .'

43

'So Mother's got to hear it from you, before he gets going. You can use what language you like.'

'I can't. It's like ...'

'You've got to, Father.'

'It'll be like – killing her.'

'Rubbish,' I said.

'You don't know. Mary and me. And you know she's sick.'

'You should have thought of that. If you want to save something, and be kind to her, you'll do it now. Before Gordon gets home too.'

I argued with him, bullied him, gave him pushes out of the yard and round to the car. Then I lit a cigarette and smoked it properly. I opened the shop.

Father did not come back. And Gordon did not come in from his train. I'd overlooked that his term exams were due to start. He had travelled home early, found Mother sleeping – her medication caused drowsiness – and locked himself in his room to study. When Father walked through the house and sat on Mother's bed, Gordon slid open his door to whisper that he was home. He expected that Father, finding her asleep, would creep back out.

So Gordon heard. The only piece of luck the Ferrys had on that day was that he arrived home early from school.

He kept them together. He put plasters on their wounds. I had thought he would be damaged, perhaps irreparably, by Father's cheating and Mother's pain, but that afternoon was the making of him. He perfected his stance. He got his sensitometer working. Gordon did a wonderful job of saving their marriage.

I've never put much credence on that phrase – saving a marriage. You pull a swimmer back from the edge of drowning and put him, or her, through the pain and indignity, the choking and

44

mucus-spitting and fighting for breath, of resuscitation and stand him up, wrap him in blankets, support him to a warm bed, feed him broth – but the horror remains, the memory . . .

Mother and Father were never the same, no matter how hard they worked at being the same. By the time I arrived home at six o'clock, Gordon had them sitting hip to hip on the sofa, holding hands. He had dinner cooking on the stove and a bunch of freshly picked dahlias in a vase on the kitchen table. He put his finger to his lips to silence me. He gave a conspiratorial wink.

Before I go on, let me complete my afternoon. Mrs Imrie came into the shop. She arrived on foot, lugging a suitcase. Although it was a sticky day, she was wearing a fur coat and a winter hat. She had several dresses draped on her arm and a string bag of shoes cutting into her fingers, which were dented from the rings – real diamonds, real gold – Jock Imrie had made her pull off. She put down the case, laid the dresses on top. Her handbag slid from under her arm and thudded on the floor.

'Alice,' she said, 'where's Earl? I've got to see Earl.'

'He's not here,' I said.

She slumped on the chair beside the door and started to cry.

'You can't see my father any more,' I said. 'We all just want you to stay away.'

'Jock has . . . Jock has . . .'

'We're not interested in Jock.'

'He's kicked me out.'

'Yes, well, what did you expect?'

'All he's let me have is some clothes. I thought maybe – Earl . . .'

'No,' I said.

'But I've got no money,' she wailed – which sent a woman at the door scurrying away. 'Earl can . . . I've got friends in Auckland. He

45

can drive me. Alice, you don't know what love does to you. I love Earl.'

'No, you don't,' I said. 'And you're not seeing him.'

'And your mother – she's not well, I know that, but a woman can't be any good to a man –'

'Don't you dare say my mother's name.'

Mrs Imrie made lip-bitten sounds of grief; and again, on that day, I felt some pity. I took half a crown from the till and went to her.

'Here. You can catch the bus.' I looked at my watch. 'There's one in fifteen minutes if you go quick.'

'I'll need . . . I'll have to get a taxi in Auckland. I can't – all this.'

She meant the dresses and suitcase.

I took another half crown from the till. For the second time that day I put the closed sign on the door. I helped Mrs Imrie to the bus stop and left her sitting there with the scrapings from her marriage. She looked at me blindly, wanting comfort, but I had none to give. I walked away, in a trough of my own at the pain everyone – yes, *everyone* – must feel. But when I looked back from the corner she had taken a mirror from her purse and was fixing her eyes and smeary mouth. She changed her flat shoes for a high-heeled pair from the string bag.

The bus driver came down the steps and helped her with her suitcase.

I opened the shop again and worked through the afternoon. Then I rode my bicycle home and found my parents hand in hand on the sofa and Gordon humming a tune as he stirred the stew.

Mother was having her menopause and doing it hard. What's the usual length of time for that bungled dispensation of release – six months, two years? Mine came like a humid breeze, bothering me, and went away after a while, leaving me cool. Hers continued for three years. Halfway through, Father had his fling – more a flutter – with Mrs Imrie.

Mary Ferry had been Mary Blythe, a Loomis girl. Her father worked in the sawmill and her mother, wiry, aproned, fag in mouth, worked at home. Slaved at home. Six children. A betting, boozing husband. She put her hands on her hips: 'It makes you laugh,' she said.

I'm sorry I lost my grandmother. She probably had other things to say.

The Blythes shifted south in 1937 when sawmill jobs opened up down there. I was eight. 'Here, Tuppence, buy something nice,' Grandma said. She put a shilling in my palm. I never saw her again.

When Father was courting Mother, he called her Merry Blythe. It got even better when they were married: Merry Ferry (and Mary Fairy now and then). She was a nurse. She dragged herself up from the six-kid family in the two-bedroomed house with coal sacks nailed over broken windows and a dunny full of wetas out the back behind a hedge. When she spoke of her mother there was always a poor-Mum sigh at the end. Of her father she said: 'Least said.' I can't remember her ever being merry. Helplessness was missing when she laughed, and any snort or giggle of completion. It was as if she decided: That's enough.

She acquired gentility along with nursing skills. She rounded her vowels, learned how to groom herself, took up tennis. The barefoot girl in the washed-out dresses, girl with flea-bitten ankles and stringy hair, became the rather elegant Miss Blythe. High-heeled shoes, cloche hat, gloved hands at ease on a patent-leather purse – I dress her from photographs but can also move around the back: stocking seams as straight as plumb-lines, curls under and over on her neck. Then I put Mary Blythe away and remember Mother: standing on a chair to dust the light-shade, blacking the stove, with her tongue stuck out. She hangs the Monday wash on the line with a peg in her mouth. But no matter how hard I try, I can't put merry in.

Mother put on weight. She refined her gentility, matching it with Father's tender-heartedness. She claimed that it was nursing people injured or sick that made her so anxious for our safety – but I believe she was afraid by nature. A slow car fifty yards away would make her clutch Gordon and me by the hand. She taught us to shake our shoes before putting them on in case a katipo spider had crawled into the toe. She ran matches under the tap after blowing them out, hid the axe behind the wash-house door so it wouldn't tempt the delivery man. But she was more afraid of things she could not name. She was afraid of losing everything.

There were times in her menopause when husband, children, house and all possessions slid into a fog of unbeing. Some of this came from the phenobarb her doctor prescribed. But there were spells when her alertness, and small measures of happiness, came back. They sometimes lasted several weeks before depression dragged her down into despair and the doctor put her back on her narcotic.

Father confessed his unfaithfulness in one of the times when she had made some steps back to knowing us and knowing who she was.

He left the door open and sat on the bed. She opened her eyes and smiled at him. Gordon listened. No one ever asked him what business he had.

Father made allowances for himself. He made a rambling progress through the seduction, left bits out, I suppose, put bits in to show how unfairly he was tempted, but the end was plain: there was a bedroom, and there in the bed was Mrs Imrie. Immovable among his circumlocutions and euphemisms, there was sex. He told her it was only once. He fell. A single time. But it was over. It was her, his wife, his Merry Ferry, that he loved. There would never be anyone else.

From the moment she understood what he was saying, Mother keened. The sound was enclosed at first, like the humming of a bumble bee in a pumpkin flower. She never denied what she was hearing. She never flashed in anger or burned him with her eyes. He held her hands tightly, one in each fist, and she made no attempt to pull away. But the sound she made grew into a wailing. Then she fought for breath, in throaty gasps.

Gordon ran in. No, not ran, Gordon stepped – like marching, he told me, to the beat of a drum (that drum his heart). He took Father's shoulders and shifted him from his seat on the bed.

'Gordon, she's choking,' Father said.

'No, she's only crying,' Gordon replied. He marched Father out of the room and sat him on the living-room sofa. 'Wait there, Dad.' (Called him 'Dad'.) He went back to the bedroom door, turned and pointed his finger: 'Don't you move.' Then he went in and closed the door.

Gordon cemented them together. He put Mother and Father square with each other – almost square, like two bricks jolted apart in an earthquake. He said the things apologists for straying husbands say: Men are like that – he couldn't help himself – it isn't a betrayal, it's just a weakness, a misstep – he'll never do it again. And much more. Nothing wise. Nothing deep. But always he returned to the essential thing: 'You love each other, Mum.' (Yes, 'Mum'.) 'He loves you.' He told her they were strong enough to step around this pot-hole in their marriage (making her smile – a fleeting smile) and move on. She must be the strong one. Wasn't that what she had always been? (Gordon telling lies.) And after all, they loved each other, remember that. They weren't just anyone, they were the Ferrys – he folded his hands together – they were like that.

Father crept across the living-room to the door. Gordon flung it open and pointed at the sofa: 'Get back there or go and dig in the garden.' He smiled at Mother when he came back. 'Dad's a bit of a drongo,' he said.

'Why did . . . Why did he . . .?'

'Because she's got whoppers, Ma.' ('Ma' now.) 'Like this.' He demonstrated the size of Mrs Imrie's breasts. 'And men like that. They're suckers for it. Mum, I promise you, it won't happen again. You're getting well. You love each other. He loves you.'

It wasn't easy. It took time. Father made tea and tried to bring it into the bedroom on a tray. Gordon sent him back to the sofa. He helped Mother into her dressing-gown and slippers and into the living-room. Shifted a cushion, sat her as close to Father as he dared.

'Mary,' Father said. 'Merry. Are you all right?'

'Don't let that tea go cold,' Gordon said, looking back from the door. Mother was stiff and Father leaning at her, repeating her name in a wheedling tone. Gordon smiled at them as if they were a picture he had painted – but that's unfair. He had just about used himself up. He went outside, walked to the back of the section, climbed to his boyhood seat in the macrocarpa hedge, sat there shivering and weeping. He made big gulping sobs, letting out his tension and his grief.

The macrocarpa smell was like a medicine for colds, bringing back memories of lying in bed as Mother read his temperature, one hundred and two, and Father measured doses in a spoon. He saw the neat rows of silver beet in the garden, the back lawn with its border of pansies. And there were the rainwater tanks on their stand, where he had wallowed on summer days after Orchard Street was linked to the Loomis water supply. He had climbed the roof like a mountaineer and shouted down the chimney to Mother shovelling ashes from the living-room grate. The little knot of Loomis town lay beyond the creek, with orchards and farms spreading out to the ranges, which stood like the rim of a blue-painted bowl.

Gordon thought: I suppose I'm grown up now.

When he was emptied and restored he went to the house. He walked into the living-room as though nothing had happened.

'Hello, the pair of you. You look cosy.'

He took the tea tray to the scullery. He chopped steak and kidney for the stew and made a custard pudding from a recipe book.

When I came in I saw that Gordon was new-made.

I found the strain of Mother being brave hard to bear and was relieved when her menopause claimed her again. She went in, came out, went in for several years. It shifted my attention from Father's adultery, which I've never thought about properly. I can't see it as much more than stealing sweets. Yet I understand the importance of trust. We must take the greatest care not to damage it.

Mother's trust was damaged beyond repair. Bravery at first, then long-suffering, took its place. Father no longer trusted himself – I don't mean not to stray; I mean to be honest, manly, honourable. He began to soften and shrink like a last-season's apple at the back of a shelf.

But they stayed together. They were always kind. They tried to make each other happy. There's no way of measuring what they achieved. The failure of the shop gave Mother a more active role. They turned a corner into that new trouble, putting the old out of sight. She worked out ways they might survive. But over several years the flash new chemist shop in Imrie's Buildings took Father's customers away. He sold his stock and closed up, and soon after that sold the Loomis house. They rented a bungalow in Westmere. Father worked on wages in a Queen Street pharmacy. Mother became a doctor's receptionist.

Gordon kept on insisting that they were all right. And, in a way, they were. But if he had not helped them set up a balance they could sustain, what would have happened, where would they have gone? I imagine them sinking and drowning, their hands just out of each other's reach. Conversely . . . But it's idle speculation. I usually conclude that they were lucky Gordon came home early on that day.

He and I completed degrees. He trained as a teacher and went off to do his country service. I went to work for the DSIR.

THREE

It makes no sense to stay in this house. After two near-accidents I've given up driving my car. The Wadestown bus puts me down at the top of the hill, then I must walk half a kilometre and climb another steep hill at the end. The final thirteen steps to my gate make thirteen cliffs, thirteen tests of my endurance. I steady myself against the rock wall, or clutch an amputated branch of the tree fern by the gate to keep my balance. If I let go I'll tumble backwards down those thirteen steps, down seventy-three years into oblivion.

Yet I'm no cot case. My great-nephew Adrian calls me a fit old dame. That's dated slang from a boy of nineteen. ('Where did you get it?' I asked. 'My grandma,' he replied. 'She used to call herself a crotchety old dame.')

I've met none of this family except for the boy. Adrian Moore is his name. (I sometimes wish he'd be Adrian Less.) He knocked on my front door one day late in summer; came on foot up the steep streets from the city, and has refused to go away.

It was the morning of my second near-accident in the car. I had not bothered to close the garage door and the wind blew straight in all night, bringing Pinex dust down from the ceiling and making the windscreen difficult to see through. I pulled the water-squirting lever and ran the wipers, and while that was going on drove through a pedestrian crossing without looking. I saw the woman yank her child out of the way. When I stopped to apologise she called me a stupid old bitch. I don't quarrel with that. Remembering the incident makes me wring my hands with distress. I almost killed a child. I said: 'Yes, I'm sorry. I'll put my car in the garage and never drive again.' I was not being humble but reasonable. I drove home shakily and have kept my word. And I don't feel reduced too much, or impoverished. My concentration might be impaired but memory and mind are as sharp as ever. I'm not ready to manage growing old the way my husband Neville did – by becoming interested in the process – because I've got decisions to make and things to do: Adrian to head off at the pass.

He's a boy who either smiles or scowls. He's not deep or devious but he's persistent. Doesn't beg for information, doesn't plead or bluster, but keeps his curiosity on show or blackens his brow. I have to stay alert to turn him aside. I can do that, but must not let him wear me down through proximity.

'Hello,' he said, when I answered the door. 'Are you Miss Ferry?'

'That depends,' I said.

I'm A. M. Ferry professionally and in the telephone book but most people know me as Mrs Kite. A. M. Kite appears in the phone book as well. (Actually I'm Doctor but I don't include that or people would be phoning for medical help.) What interested me was where this boy had got 'Miss' from. It presupposed knowledge, which presupposed intent of some out-of-the-ordinary kind. A glance told me he wasn't selling anything or doing a survey or promoting some religious belief – no satchel, no clipboard in his hand – and a closer look at his face detected no influence of drugs. One must watch for that. His clothes were unintentionally comic: beanie hat, baggy T-shirt, sneakers like boots, and jeans with the crotch at the level of his knees.

'On who you are,' I said, meaning that's what it depended on.

He took it as yes – took a handful of his beanie and pulled it off. He smiled at me.

'My name's Adrian Moore. We're related.'

'I don't think so,' I said. I have relatives descended from Mother's brothers and sister, but although I've met one or two by chance over the years none are known to me now. 'Unless you're a Blythe. I've lost touch.'

'What's a Blythe?' he said.

'My mother's family. So you've made a mistake. I don't want to seem rude, but you'd better go away.'

'No, we are,' he said, smiling again. It's a nice smile, not wholly innocent, knowing its charm. 'If I can come inside for a minute ...'

'No,' I said.

'I've got a photo that will prove it.'

A photo would be quick. It would end the argument. Also, one must look – experience the sudden blast unknown faces bring of singleness and multiplicity, of other life.

I said: 'Show it to me here. You needn't come in.'

'Well,' he said, unwilling. 'I've looked for you for a long time. Keeping me on the doorstep's kinda rude. Anyway, I'm thirsty. I got pretty hot walking up here.'

'There's a tap,' I said, pointing along the garden path. 'You can drink there.'

'Miss Ferry,' he began, but I cut him off.

'How do you know I'm Miss?'

'Do you mean you're not? Nah, you're her. You're Alice, right?'

I said nothing. I can be still, stony-faced, while churning inside. It's a gift.

'I'll give you some orange juice but that's all,' I said.

I led the way into the kitchen, breaking the rule: Never let strangers in your house. This one had stepped around it by saying my name. He nipped me with his fingers, small but tight. I had the premonition of a terrible closeness.

I took a packet of juice from the fridge and poured him a glass. His throat beat like an artery as he drank.

'I needed that,' he said. He wiped his mouth, then looked around the kitchen, delaying things. 'I'm kinda nervous, Miss Ferry.'

I almost told him to call me Alice but kept it back, thinking that although I could not deny my name I could use it as a place of retreat.

'Show me this photograph,' I said.

'You're not in it,' he said, bringing an envelope from the pocket of his jeans. 'But I guess you know who the people are.'

He opened the envelope and took a photograph out but seemed unwilling to surrender it. Instead he turned it round and held it in front of me with the top edge nipped between his finger and thumb.

I looked as though through a window at a world with the colour taken out; kept my mouth in its elderly line, although it fought to tremble and cry; said: 'I don't know them. Is this a joke?' But then had to add: 'Let me see.'

He let me take it from his fingers but stayed close, ready to grab. My eyes might hide the truth from him but told it to me: my brother Gordon. He was wearing a sports jacket and an open-necked shirt and had his arm around a pretty girl in a party dress. I knew her too. I knew the year: 1959.

'They're nice-looking people,' I said, 'but I don't know what they've got to do with me.'

'Come on, Miss Ferry.'

'Well, I don't. She's a sweet-looking girl. This boy seems to like her all right.'

'They've got names,' he said. He took the photograph and turned it over. I read: Gordy and Marl at Barb's party, September 1959.

'Marl's a fertiliser,' I said.

'It's short for Marlene. She was my grandmother. Marlene Wilkinson was her name. And Gordy is Gordon. He's Gordon Ferry. He was my grandfather.'

'Nonsense,' I said.

'So you've got a brother Gordon then, OK?'

'My family is no business of yours.'

I've seldom been so weak in a declaration. One part of my mind was asking: Adrian, did he say? I wanted to hug him, then sit him at my table and feed him carrot cake. He was – I believed it, I throbbed with belief – Gordon's grandson. It had sometimes crossed my mind that the girl would get herself pregnant. And here, in my kitchen, was a person coming down from him. But other parts – I was fragmented – cried no. I could not handle closeness; I had done without it since my husband Neville died, and even he had taken no share of Gordon. How dared this boy claim to be a part? I would not allow it; and must not let Gordon be hurt. Must keep him locked away for his sake more than mine. Did he have a 'sake'? I had to believe in it, although it might be no more than an evenness in the flow of his days.

'Gordon wasn't as tall as this. And he had fair hair.' I'm an easy liar; say the first thing into my head, then follow it up, knowing how facts strung together can confuse. Never stop at one. Don't stop at two. 'And crooked teeth. He never had a mouth full of choppers like this. He liked girls with dark hair too, not blondes. She looks a bit silly, does your Marl. A bit of a dolly bird. My brother liked serious girls.'

The boy flushed. I wondered if he might be dangerous.

'I don't mean to insult your grandma.'

'You can't any more. She's dead.'

57

'Oh. I'm sorry. Well, grandparents grow old. Was she special to you? Were you close?'

That was as gentle as I could be. I've never seen the tragedy in old people dying – although Marlene, whom I'd met once, and been clutched on the forearm by, would not have been much over sixty if she were still alive.

'She died when she was twenty,' Adrian said. 'She killed herself.'

Her palm had been warm and damp. It left a patch on my arm that cooled as it dried. She had smelled of cheap perfume and dance-hall sweat. It was as if I deflected Adrian's blow through touch and smell. Perhaps, with my mind reeling, those senses defended me. They were not enough.

'Oh,' I said: a disembodied sound. It echoed in a hollow deep within me.

Adrian sat me down on a kitchen chair. He ran a glass of water, which I drank in three gulps. Then I was able to say: 'I'm sorry. I'm so sorry.'

'Did you know her?'

'We met once. For just a minute or two.'

'Where was that?'

'In a dance hall. It was called the Majestic Cabaret. We said hello, that's all. Gordon was in the toilet. I went home when he came back. I don't think she was his girlfriend then. Just someone he'd asked out.'

'She was later on though? His girlfriend?'

'Yes, she was.'

'How come you never met her again?'

'I lived in Nelson. I was only across here for the weekend and I never came back.'

'Did he tell you about her in letters?'

'I don't remember. I don't keep letters, so don't ask.' I was

58

recovering and meant to say no more, but had to explain: 'I didn't know she was dead. As far as I knew, they broke up. There wasn't anything special going on.'

'Except my dad.'

'Are you sure of that? I mean ...'

'She was sleeping round? No way.'

'I don't want to offend you, but so long after is there any way to tell?'

'Sure. Let me ask my grandpa. Tell me where he is.'

He said 'grandpa' with such certainty, nailing Gordon down. I had no word to match it, but answered as I had to, with false honesty: 'Gordon would have told me if she was pregnant. He would have married her, he believed in things like that.'

'So let me ask him. It can't do any harm.'

'It's not possible,' I said.

'Why not?'

I looked into his young eyes and said the first thing, confident I would find whatever else was needed: 'Gordon died a long time ago. He died not long after – what's her name, Marl?'

Adrian's face contracted. It was not that openness went out; excitement, expectation went out. I felt the pain of it and looked away, then made a little moan at what I was doing. He took it for grief and managed to say: 'I'm sorry. I didn't mean to upset you.' He shrugged in apology. 'But ... If you don't feel like telling me now, can I come back?'

'How it happened? Is that what you want to know?'

'It's just, shit, I feel cut off. Him being dead, I mean. So, anything ...'

'It was a motorbike. He rode it too fast.'

'Motorbike?'

'Gordon always wanted one. He kept it in his front yard. It didn't always go.' How I can lie! 'But when it did, he took it out for spins.

You didn't have to wear a helmet then. A helmet might have saved him.'

'What happened?'

'He was going too fast round a corner and he hit a tram. But no –' I did not want blood, I was starting to see him – 'he didn't end up under the wheels. It was instantaneous.'

Adrian was silent. 'Where was it?'

'Coming down the hill from Brooklyn.'

'When?'

'1962.' The year I married Neville: it's always the first that comes to mind.

'That's more than twenty years before I was born.'

'Yes, I suppose so.'

'Dad must have been only two.'

He was lifting heavy weights out of the past, and growing dizzy with the strain.

'Sit down. I'll get you another drink.' I fetched the juice packet and filled his glass. 'What were you hoping for? What did you want to find out?'

'My father got adopted as soon as he was born. His parents, adoptive parents – well, my grandma – she didn't tell him until he got his cancer. I dunno, maybe she thought it would help. It could just as easy have knocked the bottom out of him.'

'But it didn't?'

'It got him going. He started trying to find who his real parents were. Grandma didn't know. But my dad was a persistent guy and he tracked down Marlene all right. Got her name. But finding she was dead, that really knocked him.'

'What about your mother?'

'They're divorced.'

I said I was sorry, but in fact I was fascinated. It was as if he was taking photos on an instant camera and pulling them out and showing me.

'Were divorced, I mean. Dad had liver cancer. It killed him pretty quick. Well, two years, that seemed quick. But one of the things he said was, "Try and find him, Adie. Tell him hello from me."'

'You can't now,' I said, and patted his arm. I gave myself a tick for putting Gordon out of his reach.

'Where's he buried? I'd like to see his grave.'

'No, you can't,' I said. 'He was cremated. We took the ashes to Loomis – that's where he grew up – and scattered them along the edge of the creek. It's sentimental, I suppose, but Gordon would have liked it.' I'll come to believe this, I thought. 'Look, Adrian, all this must be a shock. Would you like to stay for lunch? I was getting ready to have it when you came. Then I can tell you what Gordon was like as a boy. He was good at football. Do you play that?'

'No.'

'Well, tell me about yourself. It's not every day one gets a new relative.'

'One thing.'

'Yes?'

'Why did you say it wasn't him when you saw the photo?'

'Because,' I said – and suddenly I was crying; keeping on with my lie to Adrian, but telling a truth I'd never said out loud before – 'because I didn't want him back, not so suddenly. Because I love him more than anyone in my life.'

Tears ran down my cheeks. I blocked them with my hands.

'I've never loved anyone else, not in that way.'

Adrian is taller than Gordon by a centimetre or two, although Gordon topped six feet before he began to stoop. He's light-boned and meagrely fleshed and sometimes when I look at him the word emaciated comes to mind. I reject it because there's no hint of wasting away; rather he seems to fill himself daylong, by enquiry, curiosity, by the openness of his senses and his mind. In appearance he's a scarecrow: has put his hair in dreadlocks since coming to live with me. He takes no care of his clothes. He doesn't wash as frequently as I'd like. He eats like a horse. I'm bothered by his long neck, housing muscles, tendons, arteries, bone, passages for air and food and water, while joining head to heart, intelligence to motion – such a fragile duct for all that function. I worry about his mind, his happiness. Adrian's future has a way of consuming my past. His course can be altered by what I reveal.

When I asked about his job he said he was a barista and told me it's harder than it looks. I've stopped in Cuba Street several times and watched him at work behind his throat-clearing machine – a kind of race, a kind of dance, a trade, I suppose. The café is not the sort I go into. Perhaps wrongly, I feel I wouldn't be welcome in my silver hair and expensive clothes. It's called Outscape. The walls are painted with space girls and alien creatures in fantastic landscapes. Adrian looks at home there. One must strip the walls, still the noise, alter surfaces, but also strip, still, alter oneself to find the young – find who they are, meet on our common ground, which is, of course, as wide as our essential being. But that's no task for me. My task is smaller.

He has a huge stringed instrument: a double bass. It beats like a heart, sometimes doing just enough to keep alive, at other times excited by love or lust or hunger or its own capabilities. Adrian plays his instrument well. He tells me the bass – such an impressive beast – can't stand alone for very long. Its job, he says, is more like stitching, even when it beats hard and fast. It fastens things together: the sort of instrument, I think, Gordon might have chosen.

Adrian borrowed my car to shift his belongings from his 'squat' in Newtown to my house. I did not ask if he had a driver's licence. It's a time for trusting.

'What on earth,' I exclaimed when he carried the monstrous thing – swollen, polished, hollowed out, domineering, lovely – through the gate.

'Told you I played music,' he grinned. 'Don't worry, I'll keep it over at Massey most of the time.'

He is studying jazz part-time at the conservatorium. I went to a lunchtime concert and heard him at his stitching, delicate with his fingers, strong with his hands, up and down the strings of his double bass. Several times he played solo and people clapped, as they had for saxophone and drum solos. I could not tell whether these bits were improvised, earning applause for invention as well as skill, or whether someone had thought the notes out first. I enjoyed the concert, although some of it was too loud. It set up movements in my breathing and my blood that were quite new. There's a lot of communication in this music. It's big statement most of the time but aesthetic probings go on. Yet Adrian stayed private, it seemed. Stern-faced, he played for himself. It disappointed me. I asked him why he didn't show some emotion, and he said: 'You don't know what I'm like inside.' That's all he'll say. He doesn't want to talk about his music. It's another of the things that fill him – the most satisfying perhaps, yet it seems to cause linguistic impoverishment. I'll abide by his wish. A kind of language comes from his room when he brings his double bass home and practises half the night. There's strictness, effort, discipline and a happy freedom at the end.

I don't see much of him, with his job and his studies. He puts his board money on the kitchen table. I don't want board and every now and then I leave it there. We have a struggle, but I need the table clear so he wins in the end. When I asked him if he had a student loan he told me politely it was none of my business. So I've started a savings account at my bank. The board money goes there and he'll get it when he leaves. My present. I don't think he'll put it back on the table.

Writing that makes me frown. But I don't kid myself. When he has exhausted his interest in having an old lady interested in him – in having that outmoded thing, a great-aunt – Adrian will find another place to stay. I haven't seen signs of it yet, but the time will come. Meanwhile I behave as liking and generosity dictate. These parcels of good feeling are wrapped in guilt.

On those nights when he tells me he'll be home I cook winter stews or roast a chicken and introduce Adrian to wine. It slows him down, makes him less talkative for a while, sends him after things he doesn't always want to say. I see him pause, then make a half-blind step over his reluctance. He's not sure how much he's going to reveal. There's the bullying he suffered at school. It wasn't as bad as some kids got because although he didn't play sport he could belt out easy pop tunes on the school piano. Then he and a couple of friends formed a group and played even easier rock and roll. Adrian became popular. But he got out of there – out of the town – as soon as he could. What town? Whakatane. He had nothing against the place, in fact he liked it, but after his father died there was talk of him going to live with his mother in Hamilton and he wasn't having a bar of that. So he enrolled for the jazz course at the Massey Wellington campus.

'And here I am.'

'Tell me about your father.'

'Yeah, Dad. He was OK. Dad was good.'

It must be my cast of mind: I thought he meant morally good. Before I could stop myself, I said: 'So was Gordon.' Then I understood what he had meant: good guy, good fellow. I said quickly: 'How long were you and he alone? When your mother left?'

'I was thirteen. Hey, my thirteenth birthday, lucky thirteen. She stayed for that. Pretty thoughtful, eh? Then she moved in with the guy next door. His wife had run out on him. Mum moved in. They'd had something going, everybody knew. So Mum was our next-door neighbour for a while. Then they moved to Hamilton. Good riddance.'

'What did your father do?'

'He worked in the board mills.'

Another misunderstanding. I meant how did this man, Rodney Moore, behave when his wife left him for the man next door? But I let it lie, even though I wanted more of Gordon's son: his life, his behaviour, his appearance. I wanted to stand him between Gordon and Adrian and mark in the passing of the genes.

'When he got his cancer –' Adrian stopped.

'Three years ago?'

'Yeah.'

'When did he die?'

'December, year before last. Just before Christmas.'

'Don't talk about it if you don't want to. Have you got a photo?'

He went to his bedroom, came back with a photograph, put it down in front of me and returned to his chair.

The man was surf-casting but had turned to grin at the camera. He was wearing shorts and a football jersey and was thicker-legged and -bodied than his father or his son. I saw my father. He had Earl Ferry's brow and chin, and the same sort of hesitancy in his eye. His open, friendly grin should have belied it – but no, I saw that liquidness, that uncertainty pushed into flux by the varieties and shifts of life that Father had exhibited even as he moved into action headlong. I kept my head down and studied

Rodney Moore, feeling my father's presence and my own crypto-gamous connection.

'Where was it taken?'

'Up the beach, looks like. That's Whale Island there.'

'Did he catch any fish?'

'Don't know. He must have been about – yeah, twenty-five. Mum must have taken it.'

'Do you want to tell me what she was like?'

'Parties. Booze. Getting it on.'

'What does that mean?'

'With men. She hated being home. She hated the kitchen. Fair enough. But the guy next door was a beery slob.'

'And your father – he was . . .?'

'Kinda quiet. Mum liked music though, I'll give her that.' He was seeing connections but not wanting to go far.

'You're quiet too.'

'No, I like noise.'

'You're a quiet boy.'

It's there in him like a pool lying in a cave: the sort of quietness Gordon had when his fevers and busy-ness were done.

I asked him – these are several occasions, different dinners – asked about his father's need to know who his birth parents were.

'My grandma kinda blurted it out. She didn't know she was going to say it till she did.'

'She's the crotchety old dame?'

'Yeah, that's her. Does stuff for you, then spends the rest of the day growling about it.'

Rodney Moore had laughed and said: 'What a time to tell me.' He said, too, that his adoptive parents were his real mum and dad.

'I reckon he felt he had to say that,' Adrian said. 'I guess he meant it too, but you could see he was gone. He was filling in all sorts of things. Stuff that suddenly made sense – like why he was big and dark and they were grey and skinny. My grandma, she's got poppy-out eyes, like one of those dogs, you know, a chihuahua. She's built like one too.' Adrian thought for a moment. 'But also why they didn't fit. Like, seeing how things were and people were, and even if red was red and something round was really round.' He folded his fingers into each other. 'They could never be like that.'

'Who looked after him with his cancer?'

'Me. Not all the time. He used to go into hospital. The nurse came quite a lot. And Grandma used to come down from Tauranga. That's where they shifted. She made a production out of it but she came. Stayed a week or two, went back. She was OK.'

I tried to picture this life. My husband Neville had pancreatic cancer (adenocarcinoma). I kept on working and we paid for daily care, then it was the hospice at the end. Adrian's life with his dying father, his quotidian, his nocturnal tasks, seemed to have no edge of endurance, blunted or sharp, rather the lumpiness of good times and bad times succeeding each other. No day, sometimes no week, no month, was like the one that went before.

'What we did when he was sick was try and find out stuff about his mother. Grandma couldn't tell him much, just that she was a nurse. You wouldn't believe what Grandma said to the adoption people: she didn't want a baby from some halfwit girl. So they told her she was from a good family and a nurse.' Adrian laughed. 'It turned out to be wrong. She was a nurse aid.'

In my day it was impossible to find out who your birth mother was. It's easier now. You're put in touch, or given a name, or shown what's on the record. So Rodney Moore found out about Marlene Wilkinson: occupation, nurse aid; age, nineteen. The record did not say she died at twenty. It did not say who her baby's father was.

I asked about the photograph taken at the party. Adrian was

getting to it. Rodney Moore – I must say just Rodney – traced Marlene's parents – 'Yeah, to the graveyard. They were dead.' – then found an older sister, who wrote that Marlene had 'suffered a brief illness' and died shortly after her baby was born. She knew nothing about the baby's father and asked not to be contacted again.

'Dad had a bad time for a while. Went really down. He was getting a lot of pain and they had him on morphine. But it was her being dead that got him worst. So I wrote to the sister again and told her Dad really needed to know what Marlene was like, that sort of thing. She sent the party photo and said that was the end of it. She said Gordy might be the father, she'd never met him, she didn't know. Please would we leave her alone. So we did for a while. Dad perked up. He was still going down, you know, he was like a skeleton. Have you ever seen someone like that?'

'Yes, I have.'

'He got the idea of asking this Barb, the one they were at the party for. He'd switched to finding Gordy now he knew Marlene was dead. Jeez, I'm glad he didn't know about the motorbike.'

I almost asked, What motorbike? Felt heat in my cheeks and water in my eyes as I remembered. Adrian, far away, seeing me perhaps as only a shadow, picked up no sign of my distress.

'So I wrote to the sister again. Dad couldn't write, he couldn't get his hand to make the letters any more. I promised her this would be the last, if she'd only tell us who Barb was. Someone Marlene worked with? Some friend she had at school? If she could tell us that, we'd leave her alone. And this sister wrote back. Barb was Barbara Lisk. She was nurse aiding with Marlene at the hospital. That was all. Now keep your promise, leave me alone.'

I pictured them, the dying man, the skinny, sad-faced boy, sending out pleas and feelers from their country town, each with a little hook at the end, trying to reel in Gordon – while Gordon was

68

far away and never to be found. I would keep him safe. Adrian, though, had a flickering presence: enemy one moment, Gordon's grandson the next. I wanted him settled, easy in his mind, his way ahead uncomplicated by duty and love. He had loved (and still loved, unbrokenly) his father. His face contracted with it, then opened into a kind of innocence.

'Lisk is an unusual name,' I said.

'There was only one in the Wellington phone book. So I rang. He was her dad. Jesus, the job I had trying to make him understand. He sounded about a hundred and he was deaf. But I got an address in the end. She was Barbara Poletti and she lived in Melbourne. The old guy hadn't seen her in years. He said if I was writing, tell her it was time she came home.'

'Did he know Marlene?'

'Never heard of her. I think he hardly knew his own name. He asked me if I knew a good shoe-repair shop because one of his was getting a hole. Someone should be looking after him.'

'They probably are. You found her, I take it? This Poletti woman?'

'The old guy didn't have a phone number for her. Well, he had it but he'd lost it somewhere. But I tried the Melbourne phone book and got her first shot. Jesus, could she talk, she never stopped and I was racking up a phone bill. But I didn't mind because it was all about Marlene. Dad was listening on the cordless. We had to tell her Marlene was dead. She didn't know that. The party was for her taking off overseas, but she never got further than Oz and never wrote. She didn't know Marlene had got pregnant.'

Barbara Poletti on her friend Marlene sounds like a motorcar salesman. I mean used cars. There's something wrong with Marlene but Barbara Poletti hides it. Concentrates instead on her prettiness, her lovely curls and lovely figure and her blue blue eyes, film-star eyes. That is overdoing it. I know what Marlene looked like. She was a nice-looking girl and, as I said, she had the quality of sweetness. That sort of thing can be cloying after a while.

'She used to sing the new pop songs,' Barbara Poletti said. "Dungaree Doll", remember that? And when she was sad – and that wasn't often – "Goin' down to lonesome town to cry my troubles away". They were all the rage, those two, in 1959.'

She polished Marlene until she shone. Adrian knew straight off something was wrong. Forty years had gone by. You don't keep memories of someone you haven't seen for that long unless they're cemented in by more than a pretty face and pop songs. Some defect, some scar, some tragedy. The woman, in her chatter, was hiding it. She hid nothing about Gordon.

'Oh, him. I thought he was a goof. He was a big tall gangly boy, a complete no-hoper. He was ten years older than her too. But Marlene was potty about him. I could never work it out. Gordy this and Gordy that, and what he thinks and what he says, like, you know, pronouncements from heaven or something like that.'

Adrian, with three glasses of wine in him, becomes a mimic and a raconteur. My anger at the Poletti woman grew as he went on. I recognised nothing in her account except Gordon's tallness.

She told Adrian his name: Gordon Ferry. His job: porter at Wellington Hospital. She said: 'I suppose if she had a baby Gordon has got to be the father. I knew they were busy doing it. There'd be no one else. We weren't like these modern girls, sleeping round. And we didn't know much about taking precautions either. Poor wee Marl.'

She said Gordon had taken advantage of her. He had abused his position, because . . . a long pause here . . . 'I might as well tell you. It can't do any harm after all these years. While she was nurse aiding he never took any notice of her. But then she went into Ward 10. As a patient, I mean. He was right on to her then.'

Adrian asked her what Ward 10 was.

'It's the psychiatric ward.'

I said, at once: 'Gordon would be trying to help.'

Barbara Poletti's judgement made not the slightest dent in my certainty. Someone in a psychiatric ward, pretty girl or not – Gordon would take notice of that. He lent her books and gave her chocolates and bought the lipstick and eye make-up she wanted from the chemist – the Poletti woman admitted it, but went on to say: 'I can still see him smarming. Big long lanky thing that he was. You could see how he wanted to get her – well, I won't say where. I hope I'm not offending anyone, but he was a creepy individual.'

Adrian, pausing for another gulp of wine, recollected himself: 'Dad didn't like it. He told her Gordon Ferry was his father. He had enough left to make a joke. He said he wanted a second opinion.'

'I would have given him one. All Gordon ever wanted was to help someone.'

'But he got in bed with her in the end.'

'It's natural. Are you trying to judge him for that?'

'I'm not judging him.'

Marlene Wilkinson was in Ward 10 after trying to kill herself with Aspros. She had, Barbara Poletti said, an unstable personality. 'She wasn't mad. Don't get that idea. She just went up and down. So *far* up, so *far* down. And she was pathologically thin-skinned. The tiniest thing would hurt her. If you said – oh, "Your lipstick's crooked, Marlene," it was like slapping her in the face. I suppose you've got to say that she seemed happy with Gordon Ferry. Gordy this, Gordy that, like I said. And she loved it when he looked after her, big lanky thing. It brought out all her sweetness. She was such a sweet-natured thing. Remembering her makes me want to cry.'

Where Gordon lived, who his family were? She had no knowledge of that. She had the impression he came from out of town. Marlene said he had a stuck-up sister living in Nelson.

'That's you,' Adrian said, grinning. 'I thought you were stuck-up too, first time we met. "Get a drink of water from the tap": how about that?'

'I'm sorry,' I whispered.

'Hey, I didn't mean to upset you.'

I covered my eyes to hide my tears: Adrian, through Barbara Poletti, had given Gordon back to me. I saw him long-legged, gangling – although it was uncertainty that caused his clumsiness; saw him holding Marlene by the hand. Gordon wasn't after anything. He wasn't looking for kisses and sex, perhaps not even companionship. Everything that followed Ward 10 came from 'looking after'.

I dried my eyes with a paper napkin. 'She's wrong about Gordon. She's utterly and completely wrong.'

'So tell me about him.'

'Another time.' I did not want to share. 'Go on. What did you do? How did you find the stuck-up sister?'

He put it off for nursing his father. There was no room for Marlene and Gordon in Rodney Moore's last days. Then Adrian shifted to Wellington. 'I wouldn't have kept on with it except he asked me to. It was pretty near the last thing he said. I wasn't looking forward to it. I didn't like the sound of Gordon after la Poletti. But I didn't go too much on her either. It was fifty-fifty.'

'You were prepared to give my brother a chance?'

'Yeah,' he said, trying to see what my sarcasm meant. (Recovered equilibrium, that's all.) 'I was just going to say to him, "My dad says hello," and leave it at that. I wasn't going to do the grandson bit. Trouble was, though, I couldn't find him.'

There was no G. Ferry in the telephone book. So he started at 'A' and I came first. My snooty voice said: 'Alice Ferry and Alice Kite can't take your call. Please leave a message.' He didn't bother. Tried the Wellington electoral rolls. No Gordon Ferry. Tried the Auckland ones and the Nelson one, all the while settling into his six-person squat, taking his lessons and lectures, making endless long blacks and flat whites. It was getting to be too much, but before he put his search aside he made one more attempt on Marlene's sister.

'I did the same I did with you, just knocked on her door. When I told her who I was she screamed at me. It was like I was sticking a knife in her. She said: "She killed herself. Is that what you want to know? She swallowed pills and serves her right. She was better dead, shaming us."'

Adrian looked at me, his eyes swimming. 'Can you believe she said that?'

I shook my head.

'It was all on the doorstep. I never got inside the way I did with you. Shit, I'm glad I never went in her house.' He rubbed his hand over his eyes. 'The only good thing was, Dad never knew.'

He turned away from her slammed door and caught the train from Ngaio station back to Wellington. The gorge on one side, with the creek glinting here and there, deep down, then the tunnels one by one made an end of Marlene as a person to know, while keeping her hidden, in place; but coming into the city, rolling through the yards, opened up Gordon again. Adrian promised his father he would try searching again as soon as he had more time.

'Then,' he said, 'I had a bit of luck. One of the girls in the flat works in a library. She said to try the electoral roll for the year I wanted. That was 1959, right? And there he was. Gordon Ferry. In Ghuznee Street.'

'Number 112A,' I said.

Again it was almost too much for me. There are several reasons but I'll stick to the one I'm able to face: that corrugated-iron shack Gordon called 'my place'. It was twenty yards up Ghuznee Street from the intersection with Willis Street, and stood at the back of a gravel and weed yard behind a tin fence with a door you opened by reaching through and working a catch inside. The damp brick walls of taller buildings pressed at the side and back, jamming it deep in a cave. A place to go mad in, I thought, when I opened the door in the fence. But Gordon put his youth off there; he put himself together.

It had two rooms, one up, one down. The lavatory was outside, at one end. Must I open doors in myself; see the downstairs kitchen / living-room, twelve feet long and not much more than six feet wide; see the coir matting on the floor, the milkbar stool with chrome flaking from its legs, the bentwood chairs pinched from rubbish piled outside a house on The Terrace, the table from a junk shop, the prints – Van Gogh, Seurat – fixed on the walls with drawing pins? Gordon's dented kettle? Gordon's frying pan? His soap-shaker on the window sill with a piece of yellow soap locked inside? These things exist in a room hollowed out in my mind.

I was in Gordon's 'place' only twice. There's another room for the second time. I won't go there.

Steps went up to a hole in the ceiling. You climbed them like a ladder to the bedroom, which had a shower cubicle above the outside lavatory to share the plumbing. A built-in bed ran across the other end. It had a kapok mattress and army blankets and a junk-shop patchwork quilt. When Gordon lay down to sleep he touched the back wall with the top of his head and the front one with his stretched-out toes. A Modigliani nude was pinned where he could see it. Modigliani was daring in 1959. I wonder if Gordon took it down the first time he invited Marlene upstairs.

74

Rodney Moore had his beginning in the bed on a night (perhaps afternoon) between my first and second visits. I hope the lovers experienced ecstasy. Gordon had problems, he confessed to me once. With Marlene I hope they went away.

'I tried to find the place,' Adrian said.

'Yes?'

'It's gone.'

'I know.'

'I didn't expect to find him but I thought there might be a house.'

Instead there's the motorway exit from The Terrace tunnel. Trucks and cars belch and fume through the space my brother occupied.

'Was it a shock?'

'Yeah, kind of. It seemed like I might fill in a bit of Gordy if I could see where he lived – you know, where I guess he took Marlene. Like hitting middle C on the piano, right? "Ding", they were here. But God, the traffic never stops.'

'Progress,' I said, but might have chosen a different word. Whenever I drive through the tunnel I feel a weight of grief that will not shift until I'm in another part of town.

Adrian mooched back to his Newtown flat. He told the father living, and dying, in his head: OK, I tried. The year passed. He spent his free time as young people do. I can guess the facts but not unravel the mystery. Then his flatmate, the librarian, said: 'Is this one of your Ferrys?' She'd remembered the name for almost a year (she must like him). It was in a book called *Women in Science in Aotearoa*, a compilation of short biographies. Alice Ferry, Mycologist, gets half a dozen pages.

I told the interviewer: 'No, my private life is private, let's just stick to black spot, shall we?' She was persistent, wanting the human side. I said: 'I'm not sure I have one,' and then, annoyed at my flippancy and afraid it hid some difficult truth, gave her bits of my girlhood in Loomis: school mainly, chemist shop later on. 'So,' she said, 'you spent all your childhood in one town. In one house?' 'Yes,' I said, 'Mother and Father and me. And my brother Gordon.' I could not leave him out; it would have been denying him, and would confirm, perhaps, that I had no human side. She asked no questions but kept him in my chapter – just his name. No one but I, finding it there, knew the way to make him whole.

'You're pretty good at what you do. Mushrooms and stuff,' Adrian said. 'I looked you up in *Who's Who*. Doctor Ferry, eh?'

If I had left out Gordon I need not have told the lie that he was dead. But then I might never have known Adrian.

'Your address was the same as the one in the phone book. A. M. Ferry. So up I came.'

'He might have been another Gordon. It's not an unusual name. Nor is Ferry.'

'Nope. I knew. Soon as you opened the door. You look the same as him – in the photo, I mean.'

'Nonsense.'

'Same nose.'

'I'm an old lady.'

'Same eyes.'

I had told Adrian that I keep no photographs. He's a gullible boy, although I've begun to think it comes from honesty. There's no deception in his nature; he finds it hard to understand that others lie and cheat. I went to my bedroom and pulled out the shoebox I keep on the wardrobe floor; put it on the bed, took out the dozen packets lying inside. Family photographs kept like this – in faded Kodak envelopes, in shoeboxes, on wardrobe floors – live differently from named and dated ones arranged in albums. There's a sadness in them, a weight of knowledge not shared and secrets kept. These people have lives to live, but their lives are over. They smile through a fog of years, yet with a terrible intimacy.

Gordon's smile? It was my own. I scattered the photographs from their envelopes, paved the duvet with them, looking for one that might deny it – but nose, eyes, mouth, chin, forehead, happy look, thoughtful look, wide grin, uncertain smile were all related, all from the same set of genes, in the boy and girl. But, I told myself, he's dark, I'm fair. And look inside us. See what's inside. Then you'll know how different we are. None of the photos was of that penetrating kind. I chose one at random and took it back to Adrian in the dining-room. He had helped himself to more wine.

'You'd better go easy on that. Gordon drank too much.'

'Yeah? Dad hardly touched it. I guess I'm OK.'

'Here.' I thrust the photograph at him. 'I kept this.'

A capping photo: Gordon in his Bachelor's gown and a hood fringed with rabbit fur. He's pleased with himself, and why not? Getting your degree meant something in those days. I hug his arm like a girlfriend. I'm pleased with him too. There were times when he had wanted to run away from study, uttering the adolescent cry: 'It's got nothing to do with real life.' We had kept him at it, Mother and Father praising and pressing gently, big sister in the role of bully. I didn't enjoy it; it made me scornful of him, and more than once I snarled: 'God, when will you grow up?' I told him he had to get his meal ticket, then he could worry about real life. Now, with Gordon capped, I hugged his arm. He smiled convincingly at the camera.

'When was this?'

'1954.'

'He got a degree?'

'Just a BA. He was at training college by the time this was taken. Then he went teaching. He was at Warkworth District High School, teaching English and history. But they made him take phys ed.

77

Commercial practice too and he didn't even know how to write a cheque.'

'So what was he doing as a hospital porter?'

'He hated teaching. He couldn't keep discipline. The only time he caned a boy he had to rush into the storeroom and be sick. He said the kids loved it. They nicknamed him Chunder after that.'

'The poor bastard,' Adrian said.

'Yes. Poor bastard. So he quit. He came to Wellington and got a job at the hospital. He wanted "real life" and that was it. But see how different we are. He's dark, I'm fair.'

'Same nose and eyes though. And you're grinning the same way.' He looked again; chose a safe word: 'You were good-looking.'

'It's Gordon you're supposed to be looking at.'

'He's OK too. I guess I can see why Marlene went for him. And then, Jesus, she tops herself and he goes under a tram.' Tears in his eyes. It's more than the wine. The Ferrys and their descendants are an emotional lot. 'Why did you tell me you didn't have any photos?'

'I wanted to keep something for myself. But if you like . . . Have a look in my bedroom. There's more on the bed.'

I cleared the table, stacked the dishwasher, put the wine away. Then I waited in the living-room, in the dark, watching the luminous sea. Gordon was close, around on the town side of the hill, with another of his lost days done, another of his nights settling in. I wondered if the place where he lay down made the almost verbal welcome his shack in Ghuznee Street had made. He had told me it said hello. Was there some shadow, some whisper of that word as he returned to his 'place' tonight? I hoped so. I prayed so. I prayed for warmth and comfort for my brother.

'You've got whole bloody stacks of them,' Adrian said, coming in. He reached back and switched on the light. 'You tell some porkies, don't you Alice?' He had a dozen photos in his hand.

'Bring them here. Let me see.'

We sat at the coffee table. He dealt the photographs like playing cards.

'There's none of Marlene.'

'He didn't send me any.'

'What about the Ghuznee Street place?'

'No.'

'And the motorbike? There's none of that. What sort was it?'

'I'm no good at motorbikes. Gordon didn't have a camera anyway. Most of these were taken by my father. This is him. That's my mother. Your great-grandparents.'

'He looks like Dad.'

'Yes, likenesses.' I tapped my grandfather on the head. 'Let's hope you haven't inherited anything from him.'

'My – what? Great-great-grandad?'

'He was mean and cantankerous and utterly selfish. My father loved him all the same.'

'You and Gordon are always together.'

'That's the way Father liked it. We should have been twins.'

'So tell me about him. What was it like? You and him.'

I began: bloodless memories at first, full-blooded ones soon enough. Somewhere in the course of them I sent Adrian to the kitchen to make coffee. It gave us respite, me from letting out, almost from that physiological thing, letting down (which I've never experienced); him from ingesting. He had begun to look red and fat. Drinking coffee slowed me, settled me, and seemed to do the same for him.

He said: 'You're a good describer, Alice.'

'Well,' I said, 'I was there. But you know, when he left Warkworth, after the teaching fiasco, something ended. We shifted – all of us, I mean – on our bearings. In another way, I felt something snap. And

I wanted it to. I'd been waiting for it. I wanted Gordon to get out.'

'And he did?'

'Yes, he did. I've got nothing to tell you about Wellington. About Marlene. Any of that. I was living my own life, you've got to remember. And Gordon had his. I visited once. And we wrote a few letters. But,' I lied, 'it was gone. That –' I tapped a photograph – 'arm-hugging stuff. And the way he bends his head at me. All gone. Thank God. I really hope he and Marlene had some good times.'

'Yeah,' Adrian said, imagining. Then: 'Well, thanks. That was great.' He grinned at me. 'Auntie Alice.'

'You can stop that. I won't answer to that name.'

'But I wish . . .'

He wanted more. I wondered if it was for himself or if, somehow, he was feeding information to his father.

I said: 'Adrian, that's all. I've told you everything.'

'Yeah, OK,' he said.

'Give me those photos. I'm going to bed. You can sit up if you like.'

He watched television. I wish I could switch to another channel like that.

I put the photographs in their packets, the packets in their box, the box in the wardrobe behind my shoes. I pulled the curtains wide to let in the night and lay in bed trying to make wideness, stillness and the familiar sliding loss of the day put me to sleep; but my mind refused. Words were spoken, figures moved, events kept their colour and their darkness – all those things I had kept from Adrian. My brother Gordon walked down Molesworth Street, not knowing me.

I heard the boy use the bathroom. He closed his bedroom door. I wished he would go away, out of my house.

FOUR

I broke my ankle boulder-hopping in a West Coast creek. I dislocated my shoulder on a shingle-slide. These accidents happened
at work. A lecturer at university had tried to divert me into zoology
because, he said, botany required days in the bush and sleeping in
tents and that wasn't suitable for girls. I took no notice of him –
and joined the university tramping club – but I wasn't interested in
mountain tops and shingle-slides, or in tents and what went on
inside them; I had my sights set on 'odiferous herbs and fungous
fruits of the earth'. More prosaically, I had chosen my work.

Work grew into my fibres. Work became the equivalent of food.
Laid up with my injuries, I felt that I had gone without breakfast,
lunch and tea. My hands, my able hands, grew white and thin. My
brain was crying out: Feed me. There's a cliché about the two things
you need in life: a loving relationship and a satisfying job. I'd reverse
the order, even though I've not had both in equal amounts. I've been
in love and would have said, at the height of it, this is the very best
thing; but looking back I'm forced to declare that identifying
verticillium wilt or mosaic virus or black root rot, and finding out
what to do about them – and about a dozen other things, black spot
in apples, 'cloud' in tomatoes – have left a deeper mark on me.
Tramping through peat bogs, lying on a duckshooter's punt in

rushes in a freshwater lake, collecting algae – these come back more vividly than friendship, love and sex. Am I deficient? Is it perverse? I shrug the answers away. I'm Alice Ferry. I remember best the things that most deeply satisfied me. I say this to place myself square. I don't need to mark down my happiness; just leave it where it belongs, at the core of me. Other things, whirling in their orbits, demand attention.

As Doctor Ferry, back from two years of study in England, I joined the staff of the Harvey Institute in Nelson. There's a lot of rouse-abouting work in mycology and, at a place like the Harvey, little chance of working only in your own field. So I collected bugs and phytoplankton; I helped set up an arboretum and a herbarium; I helped with soil surveys, with our rain and sunshine gauges, a dozen things, none of which worried me as long as I got fair time in the orchards and tobacco fields and hop fields. I wrote and published papers and won myself elbow-room; I won respect. I don't mean to tell the story of my working days, but find myself compelled to record that I was a scientist and was good at my job. I'll say now how the rest of it went on.

But not how it went with my men. There's my work and my private life, and there's Gordon. My brother and I circle each other like binary stars. We're together and apart. My boyfriends – men friends, to be exact – made no gravitational pull. I amused Gordon with them – the tobacco grower, the land agent, the engineer, the lawyer. Married men except for the last, all forty-fiveish. None of them was desperate. I had a nose for desperation and kept away from it. I wanted quiet fun and relaxation and what these days is called good sex. It did not take up much of my time.

Gordon broadened himself too deliberately. Spots of puritanism remained. He told me to marry the lawyer. 'Oh no,' I said, 'I'd be

Alice Ellis.' Later on, when we'd both had too much of the flagon wine he'd learned to drink, he confessed that he'd only been to bed once with a girl and the thing had been a fiasco. His word, fiasco. 'I get too excited,' he said, meaning, I think, he was too quick.

'I had a man like that,' I said. 'I had to stop him thinking. Sex in the head is in the wrong place. Just be happy doing it. Just have fun.'

We never spoke about it again but I've an idea he improved. There were several girls between his first one and Marlene. He put their names in letters and said they were nice but never told me how he got on with them in bed. We never drank cheap red wine again.

Our letters went back and forth between Auckland and Wellington, England and Wellington, Nelson and Wellington. When I told Adrian I had visited Gordon only once, I meant in his Ghuznee Street shack. There were other times. He lived in Thorndon, close under Tinakori Hill, and in Berhampore, before his place in Ghuznee Street. I travelled down on the Limited from Auckland when I was at the DSIR, and across on the ferry from Nelson, from the Harvey. Five, perhaps six visits. Once he put me in a boarding house but the other times he gave me his bed and slept in his sleeping bag on the floor. He rented poky bedsits with landladies who didn't seem to care if I was his sister or not. All they demanded was no noise.

We talked about our parents and how we didn't want to be like them, rubbing along, being friends, putting each other first. I wanted my freedom, always, for ever, and main say – that was my term, main say – in every decision affecting me, from where I worked and what my work should be, to when to turn the light out in bed at night; from whom I lived with, and when and where, to when he should get out of my life. 'And close the gate after you,' I said. Gordon laughed. He wanted love. We had friendly fights on the subject. 'No such thing,' I declared, meaning the meaning he ascribed to it. Later, as he slept on the floor, I worried about him: sentimental still and wanting some unreal combination of servitude and grand passion. I understood how badly he could be hurt and I wished he would find some tough little girl, not too nice, who would teach him sex and human love and its limitations, and set him free. I comforted myself with reminders that he was freer than he had been the last time I stayed in Wellington; that my visits untied knots in him and faced him another degree or two towards what I described as reality. It seems odd to me now – worse than odd, stupidly blind – that I never put the weight of my love for Gordon into my debates with myself about the place of love in human affairs.

His first job in Wellington was with Commercial Cleaners, polishing linoleum floors in department stores, cleaning windows in Lambton Quay on mornings when southerlies carried sleet and hail, and the water in his bucket grew a film of ice and his cleaning rags, torn from old pyjama tops and underpants, wrapped themselves around his hands like eels from Loomis creek. He didn't mind. It was experience. He liked standing on ledges three storeys up. He liked fighting his polishing machine through deserted aisles. (I'm quoting from memory, from his letters.) His workmates named him the Professor because he always carried a book. 'Poetry?' one of them asked, looking over his shoulder. 'Yes,' Gordon said, 'but it's about a cockroach and a cat.' They don't really like me much, he wrote, but I like them OK, they're good blokes. I know a lot of stuff they don't know, but they think I'm pretty simple all the same.

He went drinking with them at knocking-off time. It was harder at first than working with them all day, but he knew about football and pretended to know about sex, so he soon got by. Drinking fast enough was the difficult thing. 'Come on, Professor, sink that stuff.' They wanted to get another round in before six o'clock.

He went to movies and plays and poetry readings, and found a pub where writers drank. He told me their names but I hadn't heard of them, and when he sent me a poetry book one of them had written I told him it was silly stuff, one dimension short. And so it was – the poor fellow couldn't see round corners. Gordon was trying to write poetry himself. I advised him to give it up. (It's called tough love these days.) I told him he had a good brain and it wasn't too late to be anything he liked, anything useful. How about a lawyer or a doctor? Gordon, don't lose your chance, I said. Be a civil servant if you like. With your degree you'd soon get promoted. You can't clean windows all your life.

After a year he took a job as a hospital porter. That was where he really found himself. Gordon loved that work: the people, sick people, the changing faces; emergencies, with ambulances sliding into the basement and trolleys cornering in corridors; then bossy ward sisters and busy nurses; and patients recovering, patients dying. He didn't mind the dying. He found it natural. He found a way – it's like a tidal shift – of emptying out death's significance and filling himself with the fact of it. Significance leads to meaning, and that's false. The fact opens compassion, pity, call it what you will, and lets one know what can be done and what can't. It brings a kind of ease. At Wellington Hospital Gordon overtook his years.

I wish I'd kept his letters. The wards and corridors came alive, the people breathed. Sickness and cure, sickness and death. Trolleys to the kitchen, lunch and dinner out to the wards, dirty linen down to the laundry and instruments to the autoclave. He carries a warm dish to pathology. Inside is a woman's right breast. He changes the oxygen bottle for a frightened girl in a tent; she mouths either thank you or don't go. A labourer broken on a building site dies before

Gordon's trolley reaches theatre. There's a twenty-stone man who needs turning every four hours. Three porters are rostered for the job: here we go, one, two, three. They hold him while a nurse changes his sheets, and 'Bastards, bastards,' whimpers the man. His skin exudes a grease that coats the porters' hands and can be scraped off with the fingernails. It's part of the job, Gordon says. We have to use plenty of soap. He's not getting hardened. He's open to whatever occurs.

One day he and Mac – a big guy, beefy, red-faced – are called to Ward 14 to lift Mr Watson, who has fallen out of bed. 'Lazy bloody nurses,' Mac says, ambling, big-buttocked, in the corridor. He gets his complaint out of the way because the ward sister will be too tough for him. She's a powerful woman, Gordon says. 'In there,' she says, 'and be quick about it.' Mr Watson is lying beside his bed, his gown, like a confirmation dress, rucked at his waist and his chimpanzee legs drawn up at the knees. He hugs his arms. His bright black eyes fasten on Gordon. Mr Watson is smeared with his own faeces. Mac bends down and snarls into his face: 'You filthy old bastard.' They lift him. Mr Watson is dying of cancer. He weighs four stone. It's like lifting sticks of kindling wood, Gordon writes. Mac throws his end of Mr Watson on the bed and stalks out, but Gordon puts his part down carefully. The man lies skewed. Gordon straightens him and says: 'OK now?' He wants to say more than that but can't find words. He can't leave the man lying in his own dirt – a foetus with knowledge in his eyes – so takes a hem of the gown and tries to wipe him clean. A nurse comes in with a basin of hot water. 'What are you doing? Get out of here.' Gordon gets. And that's all he writes to me – what he saw, what he did. The facts of it. He goes to a bathroom and washes his hands.

The next day he collects a morgue trolley – 'with a lid like those dishes where you carry in the roast' – and takes Mr Watson from

Ward 14 to the morgue. A nurse walks with him – the same nurse, friendly now. It's her job to sign the body in. They lift Mr Watson, clean-sheeted, still warm, on to a table, where the nurse uncovers his face and tightens the cloth binding his jaw. His eyelids, closed over his eyes, are too young for his face. The nurse pats his hair into place.

Gordon turns away and sees the naked body of a child on a neighbouring table.

The facts of it.

He worked more than four years at Wellington Hospital and shifted from Berhampore to his place in Ghuznee Street early in 1959. I came to see the charm of it – the seedy charm – but had to fight my sense of oppression at being locked in by an iron fence and brick walls.

I paid a two-day visit, lumping my weekend bag up Willis Street and following his instructions for finding the key in the stack of bricks against the wall: 'Two bricks along from the left, three rows down, there's an edge broken off, you can poke your fingers in and hook it out. Don't be scared, there's no spider.' I let myself in and explored.

Oh Gordon, Gordon, I thought. I could not see where he was going. A few bits of furniture, faded dusty curtains. A bent hearth shovel and a balding broom. Although they had a homely look, they frightened me instead of comforting me. Gordon's likeness was here; his correlative. His considered, his natural, his happy coming down, his settling into himself, were marked in squalor: in curling lino, dented kettle, unravelling mat. I pushed a corner straight with my toe, then mounted the ladder to his second room.

The walls were painted red. Someone had tried to make a love-nest but Gordon, I saw, used it for reading and sleeping. A single mattress and army blankets lay skew-whiff on the three-quarter bed, with a granny quilt kicked into a pile at the foot. The Modigliani nude seemed fastened to the wall for art's sake; was contemplative rather than 'take me', as though she might step down, naked it's true, and share his reading. What was he reading? Sartre. Camus. Kerouac. Colin Wilson. I can't imagine he enjoyed them. Books from which he took more comfort, I am sure, filled a bookcase screwed to the wall above his desk. He had science fiction and thrillers mixed with his old Dickens and Thomas Hardy; and poetry by people I had barely heard of in those days: Dylan Thomas and George Barker and John Donne. He was all over the place. Reading was for pleasure, not getting a degree. His books cheered me up after his downstairs room and down-and-out bed.

I straightened the quilt and blankets and fluffed up the pillow, putting off the betrayal I was bound to commit. I went downstairs for my bag and put it on the bed. I centred my nightie on the pillow, knowing he'd make me sleep up here and lay out his sleeping bag downstairs. Settling in gave me substance and seemed to give me rights. I opened his drawers, looking for more of my brother's life, believing that if it had gone wrong I was hunting for clues to put it right. I half-expected unpaid bills, and hoped for packets of Durex, but all I found, apart from letters from my parents and me, were some poems with half the lines crossed out and a pornographic cartoon: The office party after someone put Spanish Fly in the fruit punch. It made me laugh. Such busy people. I put it back carefully where I'd found it, and read my letters to him to see if I wrote well. Their tone shocked me. What right had I to lecture and bully him? I had thought I was expressing love and care but was marking my dominance. I felt a little sick at being revealed and went downstairs and washed his dirty dishes, partly in apology, partly as a penance. Then I walked down Willis Street, hunting for a grocer's and a butcher's shop. I had promised to have dinner ready when he came home.

I'm not a good cook but frying chops and boiling potatoes – mashing them with chopped onion, my idea of haute cuisine – suited my bossy contrition. I could not find a tablecloth but used two clean tea towels instead, and set the table, everything square. His little two-plate stove worked very well. The chops sizzled, with their tails curled in, while tinned peas simmered in their pot. I'd seldom been so eager to surprise. He had said he would be home just after six o'clock. I timed things to perfection. What I hadn't done was cook for three.

'Come in Cyril,' I heard Gordon say. The gate closed like cymbals. 'I'll introduce you to my sister,' he said. Then he was in the room, hugging me, while his friend stood on the doorstep. In that moment Gordon became utterly strange to me, while my love overflowed. I wanted to reverse the moment, put my brother safe at my back, reduce him to infancy and grow him again, after pushing Cyril, the creature, out and slamming the door. Forty years on, I can find only 'creature' for him. I know his name: Cyril Handy. He was fifty-one. He had a wife in another town and two married daughters. If someone took the trouble, a life could be laid out. It won't be me. He's confined to one place and a single year.

Gordon loosened his embrace and held me with an arm across my shoulders: 'Alice, this is my friend Cyril. He's come for tea.'

'Gordon,' I said, 'I've only made enough . . .'

'I can go, Gordy,' the man said. 'I don't want to cause no trouble. You feed him, missy. Don't bother about me.'

'Hey, no, I invited you. We'll make it go round,' Gordon said. He looked in the frying pan. 'Four chops. That's enough. And I've got some eggs.' He opened a cupboard. 'You can crack three eggs in there, Alice, easy eh? Sit down, Cyril. Take off your coat. We'll have a beer.'

'I could manage a beer. That'll be a treat. With your permission, missy, then I'll be gone.'

He took off his hat but not his coat, and sat at the table. Gordon opened the cupboard under the sink for a bottle of beer.

'Alice?'

'No,' I said. 'I'll be back in a minute.'

I climbed the ladder and stood in the dark in the upstairs room, trembling, controlling myself. The creature, Cyril, stood (and smelt and sounded) in my head. He was a big man shrunken to middle size. Collapses, subsidences, nasty pools and pits and rubbish heaps existed inside him. I am overdoing it because I overdid it then. Keeping to his outside: dirt ingrained in his forehead, pores open in his nose, fingernails thickened to yellow horn – oh, let me get description out of the way with etc. etc. and admit that I could not have taken all this detail in at a glance. I remember Cyril Handy – his rancid smell, his crusted grime – from sitting at table with him for an hour. His three stained teeth and yellow gums. He and Gordon got through two bottles of beer each. Gordon ate two chops. Cyril Handy offered me his, trying to scrape it with his fork on to my plate.

'Swap it with your egg, Alice,' Gordon said. 'Good mashed potatoes, Cyril, eh? Good kai.' Where had he got 'kai' from?

Cyril refused my egg. He was wary of me, ingratiating. Halfway through the meal he went outside to the lavatory. We heard him pissing, like water dribbling over a lip of moss into a pool.

'Poor old bugger,' Gordon said.

'What do you think you're doing, Gordon? What are you trying to prove?'

'He's just an alkie I met. I try to help him.'

'You can't help people like that. They don't want to be helped. Where do you meet alkies, anyway?'

'One of the guys in the pub is in AA. He only drinks sarsaparilla. He knows lots of them. He introduced me.'

'You're going up in the world then? All this one wants is money for booze, I'll bet.'

'So I give him some. But I thought if I could make him eat . . .'

'Rubbish. A mouthful of egg and potato. How much money do you give him?'

'None of your business. Now shut up, he's coming.'

'I can't stand the smell, Gordon. You'd do better to give him a bath than try to feed him.'

'I think I'll be on me way,' Cyril Handy said. 'Thanks for that spot of dinner, missy. It's a treat having a bite to eat with friends. Friendship makes the world go round, eh Gordy? Conviviality, some people call it. If I can just get me hat . . .' He picked it up from behind his chair. He was speaking with his body, with hesitations, and Gordon heard.

'Yeah, Cyril, OK. It's good to see you, mate. Hey, before you go . . .' He ran up the ladder to his bedroom and I heard him opening a drawer.

'He's a first-rate feller, young Gordon,' Cyril Handy said.

'How much does he give you?' I said.

'It isn't money changes hands, except for a bob or two. It's him and me bein' friends.'

'Leave him alone,' I hissed. Gordon was clattering down.

'Cyril, I thought you might know someone who'd like this.' He gave him the pornographic card, keeping it turned away from me.

Cyril Handy looked at it and chuckled. He shot a glance at me. 'I can maybe get a bob or two for that. You want some, Gordy? Your share?'

91

'No, you keep it. Here, in case you're short, for a cup of tea.'

I heard the chink of coins. Cyril Handy pocketed them with the card. He made his thanks – fulsome, gummy – and went away, leaving his meatworks smell.

I said to Gordon: 'That makes you feel better, I suppose?'

'No. What's the matter, Alice? What's with you?'

'Is giving him dirty pictures part of it? Are you in that trade?'

'No, I'm not. What makes you think you can look in my drawers?'

'I was looking for a place to put my nightie,' I said.

'Yeah, well . . . There's a guy who knows the guy who draws that stuff. I took it because I thought Cyril could make a bit of money.'

'He's filthy and he's hopeless and he stinks. And you'll end up like him, wait and see.'

Gordon looked at me hard. He looked in faces, sometimes in a sidelong way, for what he could find, and had told me once that what he saw in mine made him feel that everything was OK – 'I mean *everything*.' Now I thought he might burst out with anger and make denials; but soon I saw that he was measuring me. It made me almost shriek with my own denial. I was not to be known. I was the one who would know him.

He gave a little shrug, a sigh.

'It's stupid quarrelling. Thanks for cooking tea. Mum's mashed potatoes and onions, eh? Any pudding?'

'No.'

'You've hardly eaten anything. Have Cyril's chop.'

'I certainly will not.'

'I will then.' He picked it up from the plate.

'Gordon,' I shrieked, 'he was touching it with his fork.'

'So I'll get his germs. You should see what I have to touch at the hospital.' He bit into the meaty part of the chop.

I burst out crying – something I hadn't done for years. I pushed past him and ran for the ladder and clattered up. Face down on his bed, face in my nightie, I let all my anger and disappointment out. Gordon and Cyril Handy ran together – kept on morphing, is that the term? – and I kept wrenching them apart and denying that Gordon was in danger. He was simply being stupid, stupid, stupid. He was playing games. But the stink from Handy's body and clothes had risen through the hole in the floor and poisoned the room.

I heard Gordon run water and start the dishes and felt his invitation to climb down the ladder and take a tea towel and stand with him sharing the job as we had done when we were children. I refused. I opened the one window in the room and tried to get Cyril Handy out. It's clear to me now that I had fallen into a kind of hysteria, from my idea of self- and Ferry-worth and my love for Gordon, but I seemed rational to myself at the time.

My storm subsided. The night air of Wellington blew in. I got up and closed the window and lay on my back listening to Gordon boil a kettle and make tea. I knew what he would yell before he yelled it: 'No sugar, Alice?'

'No,' I called.

His head appeared and lay like a ball on the floor. 'Come and grab this.' He lifted a brimming mug, and I took it to the bed while he climbed down for his own. I turned on the light and made a place for him beside me.

'Good luck,' he said, and we clinked mugs, then sat quietly sipping for a while. He touched my face. 'You need a flannel.'

'I'll have a shower soon. If it works.'

'Sure, everything works. It's the best place I've had. I wouldn't mind staying here till I die.'

'No, you'll have a big house on a hill. With a view. And a wife. I'll let you choose the number of children.'

'Two,' he said. 'Two's best. There was a patient last week talking about her kids. I asked her how many she had and she said sixteen.'

'The people you meet. How many Cyril Handys do you know?'

'Maybe four. Yeah, four. I just have a bit of a chinwag with them. That's all.'

'And give them money.'

'Yeah, not much.' He grinned. 'For a cup of tea.'

'And they buy beer?'

'Cheap sherry mostly. So what? It's their choice.'

'Choice is long gone, isn't it?'

'No. Some of them go to AA. Cyril used to go. What have you got against him, Alice, apart from he stinks?'

'He's a waste of time.'

'Dad wouldn't have thought so.'

That stopped me for a moment, but I said: 'Father was sort of crazy. He still is. Did you know he goes and cuts Mrs Imrie's lawns? She's not Mrs Imrie any more. Mrs – something.'

'Does Mum know?'

'Probably. I think she thinks Mrs Imrie's like a disease.' Cyril Handy, I wanted to say, is a disease.

'She is, kind of, for Dad,' Gordon said.

'All he does is cut the grass. That suits him better than going to bed with her.'

'He makes love to her lawnmower,' Gordon said.

We laughed at our father, admiring him. Then Gordon asked about Tom, the latest of my married men. I told him it was over and I was finished with men that much older than myself.

'I suppose it was . . . there's always something more to find out. Things have happened to them – you know, marriage and kids. They aren't so unreal as all those others. You turn corners in them and you find something new. But then, you go round the last corner and nothing's there. They're just as empty and muscle-bound as the young ones.'

'God, Alice, what am I going to do with you?'

'Nothing,' I said. I told him I was seeing a new man, a school-teacher in his first year at the college.

'How old?'

'None of your business. Richard Ayres,' I said, enjoying the name, saying it aloud for the first time, although it carried an edge of illegitimacy, for Richie and I had only half-begun and no one knew about us yet. It was better that way, he had said, until . . . and I guessed he had a girl to let down. I did not think it would be lightly. Richie was not that sort of man.

'Remember that kid Ayres at school? We used to call him Ook,' Gordon said.

'Don't you dare.'

'Does this guy – is he for real, Alice?'

'I don't know. I think so. I hope so.'

I realised how much I hoped, and understood how helpless I was. I conceded that I was in love and at once felt a premonition of pain that made me gasp and clutch my side.

'What? What, Alice?'

'Nothing.' And that seemed right, for it went away, slid in behind the pleasure I felt in loving Richie and my expectation of more than the little – although it had seemed a lot – I had already had of him.

'The funny thing is, he's quite ugly.'

'At least he won't be up himself.'

No, I almost said, that's not true. 'He's got fat lips.' And I might have added: a big nose with a bend in it, and one nostril's bigger than the other. 'But his eyes are . . .'

'Yeah, what?'

95

'They see where he's going.' I would not say any more than that. I wasn't sure Richie's eyes saw me. 'Anyway, we haven't started properly yet. What about you? Have you got a girl?' I looked around his bedroom. 'I don't see any sign of her.'

'There's someone I'm interested in,' he said off-handedly. 'But she's never been here.'

'Slow coach,' I said.

'I won't be shooting all over the place like you.'

'I am not. I've stopped anyway. What's her name? What does she do?'

'No names.' He looked for something wooden, then touched the frame of the bed. 'It's getting stuffy in here. Let's go for a walk.'

'All right. I just need the toilet.'

'So do I. Me first.' He saw my surprise, and shrugged. 'I need to wipe it. Cyril always piddles on the seat.'

'And you let him come here?'

'He's only got half a brain left, Alice. There's a lobe missing. So...'

He climbed down the ladder and I followed with the mugs – rinsed them, trembling with revulsion. Then I used the toilet, putting layers of paper on the seat. It needed ten minutes of walking for us to regain our ease. He took me up Willis Street into the Aro Valley, then up a steep road and down – plunging down – a street with impossible bends, and back to the valley floor again. After that he said we'd earned a coffee. We walked as far as Dixon Street to a coffee shop called Man Friday and sat for an hour over single cups. Gordon talked with people he knew, while I kept antennae out for his girl. I did not like the people he introduced me to. They were either highfalutin or half-baked and none of them, as far as I could tell, had a serious job; but I admired Gordon's ease with them. Walking home, I asked who they were.

'Dunno. I hardly know them.' He waved at a couple across the street, and I saw that he had found a kind of home. It made me pleased for him, although I did not want him settling into it too deeply.

I used the shower and put on my nightie and went to bed.

'Gordon,' I said, when he came up the ladder for his sleeping bag, 'don't sleep down there. There's plenty of room.' I scrunched the mattress over, freeing a strip of the bed for him. The base was made of hardboard with holes bored in it. 'It's better than lying on the floor.'

Although the light was dim I saw him blush.

'Don't be dumb, Gordon, I'm your sister. Just lie down.'

He fussed a bit, positioning the sleeping bag, then found his ease: fetched a cushion from downstairs, changed into his pyjamas – such washboard ribs and stretched-out muscles in his legs – and wriggled into the bag.

'Not much bloody room,' he grumbled.

We talked again. He told me hospital stories and I told him about my work. The cushion was too hard, so he put it on the floor and we shared the pillow, and went to sleep with our heads joined at the sides like Siamese twins.

In the night I must have slipped down, for I woke and found my head off the pillow and Gordon's breath dampening my hair. I stepped over him and sat in a chair, worrying about his life, until I grew cold. I slid back into my blankets.

'All right?' he mumbled.

'Yes. All right.'

Towards morning he had a wet dream. I woke to hear the end of it, then knew from his sudden stillness that he had woken too. I heard him whisper, 'Shit. Shit,' and pretended I was asleep. With furtive movements he cleaned himself.

I wished a girl for Gordon who would lie in my place. I wished I could be that girl myself.

On Saturday morning we walked on Tinakori Hill, where I scouted for fungi, showing off. Who else could I be silly with? I broke open rotten logs, using my hands like spades. 'Saprophytism,' I said, and other words, until he cried: 'For God's sake find me a toadstool. I need to sit down.'

'No, look. Look,' I cried, 'here's *Boletus granulatus*. Slippery Jack. God, that's lovely. Isn't that lovely? See how it's symbiotic with the pines.' I told him how much I missed forest mycology – 'Although the work I'm doing now on black spot is important.' We walked on paths cut like ledges in the hill and he let me chatter.

When I think of my times with Gordon it's there I go most often, and although I was skiting and puffing myself and 'girling' as though I were sixteen instead of thirty, and now and then he brought me down with clever remarks, I think of it as pure, our pure time. I dream of paths made slippery with needles. Arthritic trees, purple-trunked and heavily green, stoop and peer. A boy and girl, brother and sister, amble by. They pause, they cry out, high-voiced, dis-putatious and at one. Shafts of sunlight plunge into gullies. The air is still, although the wind sighs overhead. 'Gordon,' I call. 'Hey, Alice,' he replies.

It fills me with happiness and makes me weep. I want him to have memories to transport him there. But I don't think he has a past any more, or any idea of the future; and if I exist in his mind at all it's as a simple figure, standing still, and the shadow I make lies in a pool around my feet.

We ate lunch at his place, then walked down Willis Street to the Roxy cinema, where I drew back.

'No, Gordon. I'm not going to anything as stupid as that.'

'Ah, come on. It'll be fun. Marlene's seen it. She says it's great.'

'Who's Marlene?'

'No one. Just a friend. She says this bloke gets smaller and smaller until he's way down with amoebas and things like that. He has to fight a spider with a pin.'

So we went to see *The Incredible Shrinking Man*. I sat through the early parts of it taking not much notice, thinking: Marlene, who's she?, expanding the name into a person as the hero shrank. I filled in generosity, a happy nature, but could not endow her with intelligence – not on the evidence presented on the screen. Then the picture grabbed me. The hero, who began the story as a normal-sized man – I don't remember his name or the actor's name – shortens to only three feet tall, then his shrinking stops. He falls in love with a girl his own size. She's not a dwarf, she's perfectly formed. They're standing together, they're going to kiss. But yesterday he could look straight into her eyes. Today … Oh God, it's started again, he's shrinking again; and I felt myself getting smaller along with him. I felt his horror and despair, and took Gordon's hand and hung on. After that he (the hero) lived in a doll's house. He shrank to the size of a kewpie doll. The family cat tried to eat him. A spider chased him and he killed it with a pin. Finally he was outside in the grass and microscopic creatures moved by. We leave him there …

'Gordon,' I said in the street, still clutching his hand, 'they should have found a way to make him grow again.'

'Nope. He'll be a germ. Maybe a cold germ, eh? Atchoo!'

'Pictures shouldn't end like that.'

There are times when I dream – I nightmare – that I'm only half the size of a normal person but Gordon is always full-sized. Then I'm even more reduced, many-legged, my body flat. Slaters butt into me, their antennae feeling. Or I'm deep in a macaroni cheese of fungus gnat larvae, I'm bogged in their stickiness and greed, I'm suffocating, and I wake crying for Gordon but he's never there. Sometimes I hear him laughing, as he laughed at me walking up Willis Street after the picture, and I think: It's Gordon who's the real one. I feel him in the room and turn on the light . . .

'So Marlene liked it?' I said, watching him cook spaghetti back at his place.

'You might meet her tonight,' he said.

'Where?'

'At the dance.'

'Gordon, I'm not going dancing. I didn't bring any clothes.'

'What's that you're wearing?'

'Don't be stupid. I've got no shoes. I can't dance in these.'

'I guess you won't meet Marlene then. Anyway, like I said, she's just a friend.'

I went up the ladder and laid out my good dress on the bed. I had brought it with me in case he took me to a restaurant. I'm always in fashion and always neat. It wasn't made for dancing but it wouldn't make me feel silly – just, I supposed, out of things. My shoes would do. I buy expensive shoes, featherweight, even for the street. I would only dance with Gordon once, see the real Marlene and come home. He wouldn't be able to bring her back to his place afterwards.

We ate spaghetti with meat sauce.

'I'd like to see old Cyril with a plate of this,' Gordon said.

'Don't. Don't,' I said. Picturing it made me feel ill.

At nine o'clock we walked down to the Majestic Cabaret. We paid our money and went inside and I saw at once we did not belong. Our clothes were wrong. Our hair was wrong. It made me angry, not with Gordon and myself but with the people crowded into the hall, the girls in their flared skirts, the boys with their oiled quiffs and shaved sideburns and baggy trousers and pointed shoes. They brought my difference home to me – my seriousness, which was in my nature, not resulting from age. I wanted that weightiness for Gordon; I wanted him out of this trashy, cacophonous hell – and not back in his tin shack either, but where I'd placed him in imagination: in a house of his own, with a wife and family, and working at some job with a future. I knew Gordon could be serious like me.

'Great, eh Alice?' he said, grinning around.

'I can't dance to this sort of music.'

'Yes you can.' He tried to drag me on to the floor but I resisted.

'Gordon, I won't. I can't. I've never learned that stuff.'

He saw that I had set myself and that I was more than reluctant, I was fierce.

'OK. Just stand and watch a bit. You'll get in the mood. I'm going to find Marlene.'

The music went on gyrating, hitting me with punches and slaps. Blunt and thick one moment, sharp the next, and always insistent, it forced its way into me, a kind of rape. The dancing seemed orgiastic. The girls' faces, everyone's faces, were, I thought, both eager and closed, exhausted and used. Yet it was only a few minutes after nine o'clock. What would this place be like at midnight?

A boy asked me to dance.

'I'm waiting for someone,' I said.

'Who'd want you anyway?' he sneered, and went away.

I moved into a corner behind tables and sat on a bench. I knew who would want me but I did not wish him here; I wished myself there. Richie Ayres strengthened his hold on me, and Gordon faltered, then my love for him picked up and moved on in a different gear, though seeming to have a missed beat after that. I could not choose for him or make him happy. But, I told myself, I could point and tell.

I saw him through an alleyway in the crowd, dancing with a girl in a lolly-pink dress. She's no good, I thought, she's not right. I knew it from her face, which was breathless and silly. I sensed that she was damaged. She danced energetically but was intentional, not free. Gordon was not free either, in spite of the way he rolled her on his hip and slid her between his legs and pulled her out again like a baby born. It was clever stuff. I would not have thought him capable. Yet he was treating her gently and weaving a net of safety around her – and I thought again: There's something wrong, if that's Marlene.

I came out from my barrier of chairs and waited for them at the edge of the dance. The music increased its bullying sound but I refused to let the knocks and blows stupefy me. All I wanted was a closer look at this half-finished girl and a word with Gordon, then I would go home to my own hemisphere and find grown-up people and the peace and pleasure that lay ahead for me with Richie Ayres.

The music burped like a drunkard and collapsed. My brother brought his girl to me in his branchlike arm.

'Alice, this is Marlene. We work at the hospital together.'

They were breathless and sweating and both as happy as could be. I wanted to turn my back on the girl. She had cherry lips, plump cheeks, innocent eyes, a wanting look. I sensed that she was corruptible.

'How do you do?' I said.

'Oh, hold me up, I'm going to collapse,' Marlene cried. She loosened her knees comically, pushing herself more tightly into Gordon's arm. 'I thought I was never going to make it,' she said.

'You were great. We were both great. What do you reckon, Alice? Weren't we great?'

'Yes,' I said. 'Very professional.'

'Now I want to see you two dance,' Marlene cried. 'Brother and sister dancing. I bet you'll be good.'

'I don't do jiving,' I said. 'Gordon, can I have a word? Then I think I'll go home.'

'We've just got here.'

'It's not my sort of place. And I've got a headache. I know where the key is. You can stay as late as you like. If you'll just come out in the street for a minute . . .'

His judging look again, and a weighing movement of his hand – and I knew I was in his palm, bulking large and awkward there, but that he felt little weight. I was enraged, and said: 'Gordon, now.'

'Hold on, Sis. I want to get Marlene a drink. Stay and talk to her. I'll be a sec.'

He backed away, then turned and vanished around the edge of the new dance that had started. Marlene put her hand on my forearm.

'I'm sorry you've got a headache. I've got some Aspros if that'll help.'

Her hand was damp, unpleasant, monkeyish. I dropped my arm, leaving her suspended. She smiled at me and tried again.

'He's only being polite. You can't get a drink until supper. What he's doing is gone for a wee. He just didn't like to say. But if you do need Aspros you can swallow them with water in the toilet.'

'No thank you,' I said.

'Gordon is the nicest boy I've ever met. He's the kindest. It must be wonderful being his sister.'

'Gordon can be anything he likes,' I said.

Marlene looked at me with fright.

'He does stupid things,' I said. 'Like working at the hospital.'

'But he loves it there,' she said.

'And he's not a boy. He's twenty-seven. Did you know that?'

Marlene's eyes looked for escape, going here and there. 'Why don't you like me?' she said.

'I don't know you,' I shouted, for the music was deafening. 'I'll go mad with this noise. He needs someone grown up.'

'I am. I am,' she said, starting to cry. Then she whimpered – and perhaps I imagine it, but I believe she said: 'Where is he? This is Cherry Stones. I wanted to dance Cherry Stones with him.'

'Tell him I've gone,' I said.

It was pity for him that made me leave. His sister had made his girlfriend cry – he would not know what to do about it. I imagined him sliding back and forth, and saw a bend come into his frame – love pulling on love. It was a horrible moment, which made me turn and make a cat-spit of rage at Marlene, and then made me run from the hall. I understood Gordon would love her. In her helpless way she was perfect for him.

I had gone only twenty yards up the street when he caught me by the arm. I jerked away. 'Go back. She's crying,' I said.

'What did you say to her? What is it with you, Alice?'

Again I was judged, and it maddened me. I felt so certain, so solid, so right.

'You call her a girlfriend? She's a dumby,' I said. 'What do you think she's got in her head except pop songs and ice-cream and babies and baking cakes? You've got a brain, so what are you doing with her? You know how you'll end up? Stuck in the suburbs with six kids and a mortgage and a wife who wants a new perm and nothing more than that.'

'It sounds all right to me,' he smiled. But I saw he was sad – and sad for me.

'Oh, go away. Ruin your life,' I said. Tears ran down my face. I was nowhere with him.

'Do you want me to tell you about Marlene?' he said.

'No, I don't. You couldn't. There's nothing there.'

'She's been sick.'

'What with?'

'I can't tell you that.'

I guessed something female or maybe an abortion and I felt myself sink deeper into loss of him.

'I'm helping her, that's all. She's getting better.'

'She'll marry you. That's what she's after.'

'Maybe,' he said.

'Oh Gordon, don't do that. You can be whatever you like,' I cried.

'I work at the hospital,' he said.

I looked back at the hall and saw Marlene outside the door. She was alone. She was forlorn.

'Well, work there,' I said, 'if that's what you want. But I'm not coming to see you again. I can't, Gordon. I can't watch you do this to yourself.'

'Do what?' he said.

I made no answer but shook off his hand and walked away. Cyril Handy first, and now Marlene. I loved my brother deeply, and to distraction, as people say, but he had stepped down, and away, and I could not reach him any more – although he reached me always, was always at my side. I went to his shack in Ghuznee Street and packed my bag. I left the key hidden in the pile of bricks and walked to the YWCA and persuaded them to take me, and in the morning I caught the ferry to Nelson and Richie Ayres.

Richie Ayres and Marlene. We made our choices. But Gordon had ways of seeing not open to me. I had thought I was the active one while he stayed passive.

I was wrong. There are more ways of being than that.

When I told Adrian about meeting Marlene I glossed over my cruelty. 'I was stupid,' I said. 'I was a snob.'

'You still are,' Adrian said.

FIVE

'I never saw Gordon again after that night.'

My lies are coming harder while my glibness improves. Adrian's interest subsides while mine increases. He has kept his promise to his father, as far as he can, and put it aside. For me, though, Gordon has come out. I balance each lie, each misdirection, with the repeated truth: I love you, Gordon.

I have seen him twice in the last week, walking in Molesworth Street. His head goes before him like a tortoise head. No, that's wrong, for tortoises keep their eyes front. Gordon's don't lift from the pavement. His long step is reduced to a shuffle. His sneakers, not a pair, loll their tongues. His face . . . I don't wish to describe it. Keep to the filthy quilt he trails over his shoulder and the plastic bucket in his hand. There's a beanie, like Adrian's, on his head. If he ever looks up it will fall off. The black and yellow colours belong to the football team called the Hurricanes.

I sit on the bench by the Appeal Court and watch college girls step out of his way. What does he make of their shrieking conversations? What does he make of the woman on the bench? Perhaps he sees only my ankles and shoes. They're Ferry ankles, Gordon. Remember how Mother described them: aristocratic. It's no wonder one of them broke so easily in a West Coast creek. But look higher. Please Gordon, look at me. You'll see that other Ferry possession: love.

What do I know about Gordon? Hundreds of things. And I know nothing. I don't know where 'nothing' comes from. Or remember now the source from which I collected 'things'.

A thing: was it 1968 or several years later? Was it Lyndon Baines Johnson or Spiro Agnew? One of the American oafs came on a visit. Wellington was full of his protectors – crewcut secret servicemen in natty suits. Johnson / Agnew took a ride on the cable car. Gordon – oh Gordon, what did you look like then? – was sitting in the little park halfway up, minding his business. Suddenly Americans surrounded him, cutting off his sun: big men, scrubbed, shaved to the bone. 'Who are you, buddy? What's your name, buddy? What do you do?'

Gordon looked at them calmly. The storyteller, whoever it was, says that he smiled. 'Sometimes I eat scones,' Gordon explained.

They gave him to New Zealand security men, who gave him to the police, who kept him in a cell for an hour, then let him go. They knew Gordon. They saw him around the streets all the time.

I want to tell Adrian that story but I can't.

I'm not telling him about Richie Ayres either.

Richie, thick-bodied and thick-armed. He was, in stance, as upright as a post but inside he leaned towards himself – always, in all weathers, in extremes of anticipation and completion and in acts of generosity. He rubbed his chest, a kind of frottage, while pleasing me – I don't mean in bed, I mean with a word or smile or simply with his coming into the room.

Richie followed avidity with indifference but could, if it seemed called for, overlay those primary behaviours with good humour

107

and intelligence. It was called for on meeting, on getting to know, on setting up. After that? Richie knew his women and knew they wanted more of him. I was no different. I lost myself while seeming to gain him.

He had hair on his shoulders and down his back. I rested my cheek on it like a cushion. His spatulate fingers crept on my skin, exploring wherever they pleased. His eyes, his mouth, his long, long anthropoid arms . . .

There's no whole Richie, just bits like that. I could go on and he won't exist when I've finished with him. But there's a love story too, and how can that be when there's no one with a proper sense of being on either side?

The most I can claim is that I did not let him invade my work beyond what is normal when a person is in love. He did not damage my concentration but existed like an electrical charge strengthening it: he hummed in me. Then, with my task over, he possessed me again. But I'll say for myself that without my work setting up a humming of its own, I would not have had a self to present to Richie. It saved me, in the end, from dissolution, and grew by steady accretion, like a pearl, until I possessed the knowledge, in middle life, and beyond – I have it now – that Richie was an irritant, no more than that, a piece of grit around which my proper life has grown. That's not to say my proper life is happy or virtuous, simply that it's mine, not someone else's.

Have I said yet that he was only twenty-four? I conceal it even from myself. Just like Gordon, he taught English and social studies and, like Gordon, commercial practice and physical education. He mastered those two subjects by instinct and aptitude. Richie was a better teacher than Gordon, less on the side of his pupils but more on their wavelength.

One Wednesday afternoon I took an hour off work and drove to the school in the little car I'd bought. I parked where no one would see me – Richie did not want me 'hanging round the school' – and watched the staff play the second fifteen in a rugby match. Richie was a forward. He tossed boys left and right like straw-filled puppets and bullocked over for a try, leaving his torn jersey in grasping hands. 'Hey, Gorilla Man, hey King Kong,' boys on the terrace shouted. Richie shook his fist in mock rage. He beat his chest. They cheered and whistled. Late in the game he barged at the line for a second try but opposing forwards halted him, forced him in slow motion to the ground and piled on top, all seven or eight. The backs ran in and joined them. A mountain of boys lay on top of Richie – and the mountain heaved, he forced his way out, head and arms, and lobbed the ball to one of his team-mates, who scored. The boys ripped Richie's second jersey off.

I sat in my car and buried my face in my hands. 'What am I doing?' I moaned. But I understand Richie now. He was making sure the boys loved him. He knew what he was about.

The way to get what he wanted from me, which wasn't love, was to treat me like dirt. I've thought a while about that phrase. It's not a lazy choice and it isn't easy. I mean women were base material. I was the handful he had picked up – and better quality than he'd found before: no clay in the mixture, good rich soil. So, for a while, Richie cultivated me.

It's an absurd metaphor and doesn't hold up. But the truth in it is that I began to feel like something he held in the palm of his hand and ran his thumb through to feel the texture. I knew that he could toss me aside any time he wanted, so I worked at being more and more the thing lying in his palm. I practised the Alice Ferry who pleased him most. So I'll let it stand.

I rented a flat in Nile Street, with the Maitai River running at the bottom of the garden. I sat on the bank in the evenings, or on weekend afternoons when Richie did not want me, and heard the water sliding over stones. I admired its silkiness and the easy turning with which it found its way. A child floated by on an inner tube. He smiled at me as though I were part of the world. Those times were like an argument against Richie, stronger than the arguments of friends, who deplored him, found him the rudest, most arrogant etc., saw that he was using me and ruining me, saw that I was ill with him. A trout, speckled on its back and cream on its underside, held itself in the current by the flicking of its tail. It told me I should free myself from Richie. It lived entirely in its element.

I opened my book and took up residence for a chapter or two. I thought about work and how I might publish my next paper without the Harvey director adding his name. I worried about Gordon for a while. His letters were friendly and full of chat (he had bought a motorbike and something had gone wrong with it, he couldn't get it started) but said nothing about Marlene and nothing about him and me. I cooled my feet in the water, listening to radio music over two hedges – a flute breathing and a harp plinking – so on, so on, afloat above my yearning for Richie Ayres.

I was driving to his place that evening to cook dinner. Before perhaps, but certainly afterwards, we would make love. I would creep out of his bed at four in the morning. and drive home, careful not to wake or compromise him. I was a woman of thirty who had had, and used in her way, half a dozen lovers. I was helpless in Richie Ayres' hands.

His flat was in Tahunanui, close to the beach. I drove there at six o'clock, with T-bone steaks bought the day before and a bottle of Chateauneuf du Pape supplied by a publican who thought it was plonk (he showed me a dusty case in a backyard shed and told me to suggest a price. We settled on one and six a bottle). I meant to surprise Richie and wanted him to say how clever I had been. The sun was setting behind the Arthur Range. Huge grey clouds turned purple and red. I hurried up his path under rhododendron trees, with agapanthus leaves stroking my thighs. I was hot with anticipation, and was a little mad. I meant to drag Richie to the window, show him the black mountains and the tumorous clouds, then slide my hands inside his shirt, round his furred back, and take him, wrestle him into his bed. Wine afterwards, steak later on.

The flat was dark. He had thumb-tacked a note on his front door: Sorry Alice, had to go out. Might see you tomorrow. R.

I can hear the sound I made: a bat-shriek of diminishment and despair. The sky darkened and pressed me flat. I believe that for a while I lay insensible on his porch. Later I found myself sitting on his doorstep, and there I stayed, hour after hour, ten o'clock, midnight, two o'clock. I shivered. I hugged myself smaller and smaller, I shrank like the incredible shrinking man, and held on to a sense of my being only through glints of light from the moon and through attenuated sounds: waves slapping on the sea-wall, hissing on the beach, a girl far away laughing like a bird. It was like the consciousness that's left when you know – but barely know – your nightmare is a dream, when you hear the distant whisper: I can wake up.

Three o'clock. I slid from one side of myself to the other. Richie was coming; he would not come. I should be ready for him; I should be away and showing no anxiety or bother. I hated him. I loved him, needed him, had to have him. Psychic orgasms, psychic murders, tormented me. Finally, knowledge that I was a mess drove me away. He must not see me ravaged and swollen-eyed.

I left the bottle of wine on his doorstep and fled in terror. On the way home I stopped the car and threw the T-bone steaks into the sea. Exhaustion should have stopped me cold after that, but I could not climb into my bed. He enveloped me, he was wrapped around my mind. It was instinct that took me down the cold lawn to the river. I would lie in an element not mine. I would be a fish. In my nightclothes I sank into the water, not to drown but to be other than myself. I did not go in deep but let the current bounce me on the stones. Every cold touch was a washing free. I entered a kind of sleep, half in my body, half in my mind, and each half stopped the other from floating away.

It seemed to me that hours passed. I looked for the dawn as I walked dripping to the house, but the clock in the kitchen had moved less than ten minutes. I would have died from hypothermia otherwise. I stripped off my nightie, wrapped myself in my eiderdown and went to bed, dived into sleep. It was mid-morning before I woke. I sat up and yawned and stretched my arms. My mind was empty. I put my feet on the floor, and then, two-legged, upright, back in my life, said: 'Richie. Where is he? Where are you, Richie?'

There are ways to free yourself from obsession. I came close but he was too strong.

I waited for him in my sitting-room, wrapped in my chair. Neville Kite walked past the window. I heard him knock, heard him call my name, then saw him back at the window, peering in with his hand shielding his eyes. It took him a moment to find me, then his look bored into me and he understood. He went back to the door and let himself in.

'Alice? Are you all right?'

I made no answer and he took my shoulders and rocked me gently back and forth.

'Alice. Come on, girl, pull yourself together.'

I told him to go away, I was expecting a friend.

He crouched in front of me and made me look at him. 'No one's worth it,' he said. 'No one's worth drowning in. Believe me, Alice.'

If I could have spoken I would have told him it was no good talking like that. Neville had no entry to my world – my grey thin world thickened into life by Richie Ayres. Neville was a wind-up toy whirring with clockwork sounds and moving with mechanical steps, jerkily. I told him again to go away. Instead he made me a cup of tea. Years later, when we were married, he apologised for putting sugar in it. He never apologised for refusing to go, even when I screamed at him – 'Get out of my house, you stupid old man'; even when I threw my tea at him. He got a towel from the bathroom and dried his face, then wiped the back of his chair and the wall behind it.

The tea had gone cold by the time I threw it. 'No,' Neville used to remind me, 'lukewarm.' Shall I say now who he was? Just the bare facts because Richie still has two months to go. Neville Kite, entomologist, lepidopterist, conchologist, soil chemist: all-purpose scientific man. He was twice my age when I married him. We did the arithmetic and it worked out almost to the day. He was older than my father – but oh how like a boy Neville seems when I stand them together in my mind.

He had little schooling; left when he was fourteen, learned his science on the job, and became the best entomologist the Harvey ever had – published more papers, did more work, helped everyone, as well as being our jack-of-all-trades, our maintenance man and encyclopaedia. Yet there were scientists in the place, young and old equally, who were scornful of him because he had no qualifications. 'No. None. Not even School Certificate. I think I came top in nature study at Central School. And I won the sack race.'

The day I arrived at the Harvey, the director, a pompous, lazy, ambitious fellow called Doctor Staines (who pinched other people's research) took me round the labs and offices to meet the staff. 'We needn't bother with Kite,' he said, passing an open door where a man in a white coat with the sleeves too short was poking at something under a microscope. Neville's whisper followed us down the corridor: 'No schooling at all.'

I went back and introduced myself when the tour was over. Neville was dissecting out the stomach of a sandfly.

'Why?' I said.

'To see if I can do it. Have a look. This one's empty. He must have been trying to feed on our director.'

We became friends – better than friends, intimates. He learned most of my secrets. He watched my bad behaviour with understanding one day and bafflement the next. My need for love, if that's the word, with fortyish men was explicable. He said he thought he could see what I was chasing, but didn't it lie off the mainstream of experience? He did not want to generalise, was dead against it, but people could not be happy in dead-end streets. There must be a view into the distance. He carried on but stopped before I grew bored. Neville made me think for myself, and made me laugh – something Richie was never able to do.

Shortly after I threw my tea at Neville, Richie arrived – walked straight in. He never knocked. He said: 'Gidday, Doc. I hope you're leaving.'

'It's Mister, not Doc, my boy,' Neville replied. 'Alice, would you like me to stay?'

'No, go. Please go.'

He took the tea-stained towel with him and left it in the washhouse.

'What did he want?' Richie said.

'Nothing. He just came on a visit.'

'The old bugger wants to get into your pants.'

I used to believe Richie invented that phrase. It amuses me when I hear it – knickers, pants – for it reminds me how little Richie knew, what a simple organism he was. I'm not saying he was wrong about Neville, but he could not begin to imagine the other things 'old goat balls' wanted with me.

'French wine,' Richie said, holding up the bottle.

'Only one and six. He didn't know.'

'Smart girl. Got a corkscrew?'

I fetched it and we went on from there. I did not ask where he had been the night before. I made no reproaches, but boasted that I'd gone for a midnight swim in the river. I tried all ways to be the one, and there were moments when I almost settled into focus for him. That afternoon was probably the closest I came. We made love many times and I spoke soundlessly as he slept from his exertions: This is the very best thing. I put my lips against his ear and whispered: 'I love you, Richie.' Repeated it, repeated it, believing it might work subliminally and echo back with his name changed to mine – 'love you, Alice' – if I tried harder, kept on trying.

'Love you, Richie.'

I laugh angrily as I think of it.

There's little more to say about Richie Ayres. Well, his muscular rudeness, his quick brain, I could add a dozen little paired-off things like that, but in the two months we had left his infinite carelessness of me was the thing I learned.

End of term was coming at his school. He would spend Christmas in New Plymouth with his mum and dad. I understood that (I was going nowhere; I did not want to be with other people, which was how my family appeared to me now), but I begged to meet him afterwards. I'd take my holidays and some unpaid leave and we'd go where we could be by ourselves.

'Hey, take it easy. I'll let you know.'

But it was the Harvey secretary, Bonnie Haley, who let me know. Her vein of malice was buried deep but little chipped-off bits emerged as snide merriment.

'He's a popular boy, your Mr Ayres.'

'He's not mine.'

'There's weeping and wailing up there.'

'Where?'

'At the school. He'll leave a big gap. But I guess you can't pin a young man down. Not when he's as fit and spry as Mr King Kong Ayres.' She smiled at me. 'You didn't know? He's given notice. He's leaving at the end of term.'

I turned to go. She called after me: 'My boy Darryl's in his form. He broke it to them yesterday.'

And would not have broken it to me until he had squeezed every last drop out.

I drove to Tahunanui and waited on the footpath outside his flat. Trucks like roaring beasts went by, followed by hooting sedans; then Richie cycled through the misty rain, wearing the black slicker that fitted him like a carapace. He dismounted and made a flat gesture with his hand, slicing me out of his day.

'No, Alice. Not now.'

I followed him up the path, pleading at first, then screaming at him, and he hurried me, bundled me inside and slammed the door.

'You stupid bitch. I have to live here.'

'Richie, you didn't tell me. I could have finished my job too . . .'

I won't put it all down, it's demeaning. Just say that he told me he was getting out of teaching for good. He had worked out his bond: 'Thank God I only had it for one year.'

'But you're not leaving Nelson?'

'Sure I am. Why would I stay in a one-horse town? OK Alice, I'm going overseas. I'm booked on a ship called the *Castel Felice*, leaving Auckland at the end of January. Think of your boy in London, eh? They'll know I've arrived.'

'But I can come. I can buy a ticket.' I told him we'd get married and see London together. I had lived there. I would show it to him – Hyde Park, Tower Bridge . . .

'Have you ever heard me say the word marriage?'

'I thought . . . I thought . . .'

'Well you thought wrong. Do you think I'd saddle myself with a wife six years older than me?'

I must have looked like a fish, my mouth opening and closing, and no sound coming out.

He said: 'God, Alice, you should see yourself. Why don't you go in the bathroom and clean up? Then we'll have a farewell one. What do you say? One for the road.'

I backed away from him, and heard him say: 'I've been doing you a favour, Alice.'

I ran down the path, got into my car. I don't know how I drove home without crashing. Then I was sick, both ways: down on my hands and knees on the kitchen floor, retching time after time; and sick in my head for months after that.

I never saw Richie Ayres again. What poignant words, what an echo of grief – except that I'm inclined to cheer. And in fact, last year, I did see him. We passed in Lambton Quay, and what a barrel of a man he had become at sixty-five. What a pug-dog, hungry, empty face. He's Sir Richard – squeaking in before the Labour government got rid of 'Sir' – for his career in property. But enough of him. We passed in the street, as in life, and went our ways. I saw him first and blanked my eyes; saw him recognise me and felt the little blow my non-recognition dealt. I scored a hurt to his self-esteem. It elated me. I walked on smiling and never looked back.

There are better people than either of us walking the Wellington streets.

I'd like to describe my life as Dr Ferry and Mrs Kite but have a bridge to cross before I reach it. I'll call my sickness by the name my doctor gave, nervous prostration, and change the metaphor from bridge to plain, or desert perhaps, a sandy waste. I stumble into pits of amnesia recalling it. How did so many months go by? What did I do all day? I wasn't simply lying in bed. I've some memory of the people who cared for me, Neville especially; and I remember river picnics and bush walks when I became almost happy. Then Richie struck in me like a gong and his terrible dark vibrations sounded on and on and on . . .

What else? Another dark sound started in that time, but this one reverberates still. It is ten o'clock in Wellington. The weather is windy but dry. Gordon has filled in for a night-shift porter whose car has broken down. He takes a bus from the hospital to Manners Street, then walks up Willis Street and round the corner into Ghuznee Street. Men stand in a group outside his place, where two police cars seal off the roadway. I see him in the overhead light, frozen in mid-step, weakened, unmade. The image sits in my skull, vibrating like a cymbal. He changes from Gordon then into Gordon now.

He runs up the street. A policeman stops him at the gate in the iron fence. 'I live here,' Gordon cries. He sees men crouching by a body on the ground. 'Who is it? Is it Marlene? *Marlene*,' he shouts.

I don't go forward from there; I go back to the Willis Street corner and Gordon's face. Always, that is where I go. There are pits of forgetting on either side. Some protective force is responsible. I don't believe I dug them by myself.

Father telephoned from Wellington. He and Mother had flown down from Auckland to be with Gordon, and they wanted me to come across. The call came in the morning, to the Harvey, and Bonnie Haley, supposing, perhaps knowing, more than she should, fetched Neville Kite to the telephone. He told Father I was not well, then admitted it was serious; I was off work and no one knew when I would be back – but friends, good friends, were looking after me . . .

I had talked with Neville about Gordon several times, describing his innocence and carelessness and his unfitness for 'getting on', then his silliness with the girl, Marlene (denying fiercely to myself my own silliness with Richie Ayres). I explained how close we were and how I loved him. Neville understood all that, perhaps as well as I. He asked Father what had gone wrong.

'The police found a body in his yard. Stabbed to death. They don't suspect Gordon. He was at work. But of course he's terribly upset.'

'I read about it in the paper. I had no idea it was Gordon's place,' Neville said.

'So Alice knows?'

'I haven't seen her this morning. But I don't think you should tell her about this. She's not well enough.'

Mother hurried across the strait to nurse me. Father stayed with Gordon. They, poor innocents, made things worse. Gordon was in a state like mine. Every word Father spoke, each closeness he attempted, pushed him further away. 'I couldn't get near him,' Father complained for the rest of his life. As for Mother, she sat by my bed and talked and talked; she followed me from the sitting-room to the kitchen, to the bathroom, to the back porch, declaring: We'll do this, we'll do that, and Gordon too, when you're well, when you've both pulled yourselves together. I sat by the river. She followed me. If I had walked in and floated away she would have floated by my side.

Neville troubled Mother. He was not only older than me, he was older than her. 'We're only friends,' I think I said, and he must have said the same. She never believed it. She came to think my sickness had something to do with the unnaturalness of 'liking' an old man.

'I don't "like" him,' I said. 'Mother, go away.'

When I gained sufficient strength to move from pleading with her to ordering, she obeyed: went back across the strait to Father. By that time she had told me what happened at Gordon's place. I shifted side on to it and would not look. It fell into pits of unknowing, dug by the force I've already mentioned (benign, and, I must acknowledge now, part of me), and stayed there while I got well from Richie Ayres.

Here are some of the things that took place on the night of the murder, reconstructed from Mother's account and from information I collected later on:

Gordon agreed to work until the night-shift porter arrived. He caught Marlene going off work and told her he would not be able to see her that night.

'Why don't I go to your place and wait?' Marlene said.

'I'll have to send you home in a taxi,' he said.

'I might stay all night. Now you're blushing.' She stood on tip-toes and kissed his cheek. It's my guess she meant to tell him she was pregnant. He would have been pleased: that's more than a guess.

Marlene walked home from work and ate dinner, then put on her pretty clothes and applied her make-up. She told her mother she was going to the pictures. Her parents worried about Marlene: she had been unwell and seemed too carefree suddenly.

'Where?' her mother asked.

'Oh, the Roxy,' Marlene said.

'Who with?'

'Some girls from work. They might ask me to stay the night.'

She walked from Mt Victoria and arrived at Gordon's place about half-past eight. The dark yard made her nervous but she carried a pocket torch for the key in the pile of bricks. She shone it along the path to his door, then over his broken motorbike by the lavatory and along the foot of the wall to the yellow bricks. ('Gordon says she always sings that "Follow the Yellow Brick Road",' Mother said. 'He wrote us letters about her. He's serious.')

Marlene put her finger in the hole and hooked out the key, then shone the torch on the door again. Something dark and long, without a shape, lay hard against the building on the other side. She turned the torch on it and cried out. A man was sleeping there with his face turned to the sky. Marlene ran to the gate. She pulled it open and let it bang behind her. (Gordon had fitted it with a spring.) The footpath was empty but cars going by in Willis Street made her less afraid. She supposed some drunk had stumbled in and gone to sleep, and after a moment she worked up courage to open the gate and shine the torch again.

'Hey, you,' Marlene said.

'This is private property,' she said.

She thought she might go close and poke him with her toe. First she propped the gate open with a stick Gordon had broken from a tree. She kept the torch on the man's face as she approached, and halfway there saw who it was.

'Mr Handy, are you all right?' Marlene said.

She went a step closer. 'Mr Handy, wake up please.'

She wanted him out of the yard before Gordon arrived and felt in her pocket for a florin she could give him. Then she wondered why she could not hear breathing, and she walked the last steps quickly and peered into his face. His eyelids were half open, showing only whites. His mouth had a yellow tongue curled at the back. Marlene put down her torch and tried to feel his pulse but a dirty bandage around his palm put her off. His other arm was jammed against the wall. She put her hand inside his overcoat to feel his heart. Her fingers paddled in blood lying pooled in the incurving bones of his chest.

Marlene looked at her hand by torchlight. She ran out the gate and screamed: 'Help me. Help.'

A man in the street asked what was wrong.

'There's a dead man in there,' Marlene cried.

'There's blood on you. Jesus, I'm getting out,' he said.

Marlene ran to the corner. 'A dead man,' she cried to people walking by.

'Where?'

'Inside that gate. I've got to find Gordon.'

She ran across Willis Street and down Ghuznee Street, trying to reach him at the hospital. In Taranaki Street she tripped and fell, and stayed, panting, weeping, on her knees. People stopped to help. They saw blood smeared on her snow-white blouse. Someone called the police.

Things grow confused. Marlene keeps repeating that she must go to the hospital. She tells the constable who arrives that there's a dead man in a yard in Ghuznee Street. He takes her to the station, where the sergeant calls a doctor. I don't know all the ins and outs. Several people venture into Gordon's yard and peer at the body. By the time the men who investigate murders arrive they know about the woman with blood on her clothes. Shortly after ten o'clock, Gordon runs up the street. They don't need him to identify the body. Cyril Handy the vagrant has been in and out of the cells for fifteen years.

But other questioning goes on and on. They ask him, they ask her . . . What is Handy doing in Gordon's yard? How does he know him, how well does Marlene know him, and what was she doing there anyway? Hundreds of questions, but always coming back to: What about the blood, Marlene? Where did you put the knife?

The doctor put a stop to it and Marlene's parents helped her from her chair to take her home. Gordon passed by in the corridor. She tried to run to him, and they called each other's names, but Marlene's father blocked the door while policemen hustled Gordon into another room.

They never saw each other again. There's no hollow sound in those words: they're sharp and hard. Using them, I see Marlene's face as I saw it when she came to me, smiling, in the dancehall: her happy cheeks and plump mouth and eyes as blue as a baby's rattle, and behind all this I see, and sometimes seem to hold in the palms of my hands, her hurt mind. I hold Gordon too . . .

'He can't get over her. He can't seem to get her out of his head,' Mother complained.

I turned my face to the wall. 'Go away,' I said.

I'll finish with the Cyril Handy case. Gordon was never a suspect. He had been at the hospital from eight o'clock in the morning until more than half an hour after the body was found.

The police were not able to question Marlene again. She lapsed from her hysteria into silence. No one could bring her out. She stopped saying even Gordon's name. But several people had seen her walking from Mt Victoria to Ghuznee Street. She had often gone with Gordon to the Man Friday coffee shop in Dixon Street. Friends there had run out and stopped her as she walked by. They talked for several minutes. Marlene was happy; she was 'chirruping', one of them said.

According to the pathologist, Handy had probably died while Marlene was at dinner, on the other side of Wellington, more than a mile away.

The killer has never been found. The crime does not get into books of unsolved murders. It's not dramatic enough or puzzling enough, and Handy is unimportant. There are girls who hitchhiked and were never seen again. There's a caretaker blown up with a bomb and a drug dealer shot in the head and burnt in his car. Who is Cyril Handy?

And who is Marlene Wilkinson, who is Gordon Ferry? They are wiped out from public consciousness too.

SIX

Adrian is nervous about inviting his new girl home. I don't blame him, after the last. That was Tessa – now, I'm pleased to say, past tense. I make the judgement without animus. They grated against each other. None of their intimacies, of word and touch, were convincing. It was, I think, simply a matter of going through the motions. (In these days of free behaviour there's just as much expected of the young as there was of us, in a different way, fifty years ago.) They grated even in their music.

I went to another concert; enjoyed it less but enjoyed Adrian more: his cleverness, the way his left hand ran up and down the neck of his instrument, as quick as a spider, while his right plucked and beat out lovely deep-throated sounds. The double bass sometimes looks dropsical, and Adrian, so tall and thin behind it, seems to massage strength into it with one hand and draw contentment out with the other. There's something medical too in the wires that snake away – from drums and guitars as well as the bass. It seems you can't make music today (Adrian's sort) without electronic help.

When he asked my opinion of the singer, I said: 'Do you really want to know?'

'Sure.'

'Awful,' I said.

Adrian has tell-tale cheeks, tell-tale eyes. He blushed and flashed. 'That's balls, Alice. You don't know zilch.'

'Well, it's such hard singing. Such a hard voice. And she's flat. She's out of tune.'

'Tune,' he sneered. 'It's jazz singing, it isn't pop.'

'Perhaps it's just the acoustics there. I didn't like it, Adrian. But she's pretty, if that's what you want me to say.'

I asked her name but he was offended and would not tell me. All the same, he brought her home several weeks later, for practice, not for a meal, and she was such a sweet, eager thing – no hardness in her – that I felt a skein of grief and guilt twisting inside me all through our meeting. Not that she looked like Marlene, not in the least. A tall girl, brown-eyed, all her bones on show. She was breathless with me and I could not imagine where the hardness in her singing came from. With Adrian, though, she was bossy, flinty at times; and he with her. I saw they liked each other in the way young people do, but would strike too many sparks to stay comfortable beyond a week or two.

Let them go, I thought, they'll get to the end.

She sang her tuneless songs in his room, while he played unamplified. They stopped and started, repeated things, and shouted at each other now and then, sometimes good-humouredly, sometimes not.

I caught Adrian in the kitchen before I went to bed. 'I don't mind if she stays the night.'

'You mean it?' he said.

'Yes, I do. It's your room, Adrian, and your friend. I live at the other end of the house.'

Tessa lasted longer than I'd predicted. She came and went, and I grew bored with her. She, I'm afraid, grew bored with Adrian. He was serious about his music and demanded the same of her.

So: quarrels. She wanted more movies, more clubbing, more fun. She screamed at him, from his room, that he was 'so fucking intense'.

'She's gone,' he said to me one day.

'Where?'

'Given up her course. Gone home. You were right, she couldn't sing.' He tapped his head. 'She didn't have it up here.' Then he almost put his hand on his heart – or here – but decided he wasn't sure of what he meant.

Now there's Bets – a no-nonsense shortening of Elizabeth. Adrian got over his nervousness and brought her home. Bets is a different kettle of fish. I won't call her a girl. This woman knows who she is and what she wants.

I don't like it that she's six years older than Adrian. I don't like the echo it sounds. I don't like it that she wears op-shop clothes and rings in her eyebrows and a stud in her nose. I said: 'Don't those things hurt?' and she replied: 'I wouldn't wear them if they did. I'm not silly.'

'Are you doing a music course too?'

'No, I'm not.' She was keeping it open whether to like me or not.

Adrian frowned at what was going on. 'Bets is at the Learning Connexion,' he said.

'Oh?' I said.

'The art school out at Island Bay.'

'Ah yes, I've heard of it.' Heard it described as a school for dropouts and failures. 'What sort of painting do you do?'

Adrian again: 'She's a conceptual artist. She does installations.'

Washing machines get installed. Television aerials, I thought. 'So, found objects? That sort of thing? Do you go to the tip?'

'There's a bit more to it than that,' Bets said.

I don't hold it against her that she's plain. I hold it against her that she reminds me of me. She's too direct – upfront, in Adrian's language. Two of us doesn't make for comfort. Our difference is: she says the first thing into her head, I say it after a pause for calculation.

'Where's the toilet, Adie? I need to pee,' she said.

'Where did you find her?' I asked when she had gone.

'Lay off, Alice. Just give her a chance.'

'I don't want her staying the night.'

'She wouldn't want to. Now shut up, here she comes.'

I believe the woman hadn't washed her hands. She has, though, a healthy look, a kind of animal clean-ness. She's as tall as Tessa but well filled out. Nice body, very (I imagine) holdable. Her plain-ness is in her face, which is broad and somewhat slabby. The angles don't meet properly. Eyes clear and straight, upfront and to the point. She shouldn't wear her hair tied at the sides in that childish way. Yellow hair that Mrs Imrie would have been able to do things with. The stud set in the flange of her nose looks like a pimple.

I got the impression that alongside speaking out she was studying me, turning me round, perhaps with the part of her mind that makes her do art. She wants to put me in an installation.

'So why have you got two names, Ferry and Kite?'

'One's for my work, and I loved my work, I was good at it. The other's for my husband. I loved him too.'

'What's so special about mushrooms? Can you spend your whole life looking at them?'

I don't bend to silliness of that sort. 'If you challenge me on fungi, Bets, I'll tie you in knots so tight you'll never get out.'

'Yeah, Bets, can it,' Adrian said.

The woman grinned. 'All right, tell me,' she said.

Her clear eyes and quick smile and nods of interest make her seem uncritical, but inside, I've come to see, she processes like mad. I like putting my working self in front of people. It's like pulling documents up on a screen, having this part, then that part of my life returned to me. It's like having colours flash into being one by one, red, yellow, green, blue, until the spectrum is complete and there's an Alice Ferry rainbow in the sky. I feel so pleased with myself. And I think, as I talked, that Bets, with a reservation or two, began to like me. She certainly liked to hear about a woman succeeding in a man's world; clapped her hands when I described how I'd 'fronted up' to Doctor Staines and told him to keep his paws off my research, and his name off my papers, or I'd tell the world how little he really knew about black spot.

I didn't stay long at the Harvey after that. Neville and I went to Auckland, where I worked for the DSIR again, in limnology as well as mycology. I lectured in the botany department at the university and if I'd joined full time would have been HOD before I retired. But I liked fieldwork too much for that, and lab work too, and prying deeply. Creeks go on and on, winding to the sea, and lakes spread out, and some are alive like animals in their natural state and some are dying in a kind of captivity. I followed them and sampled them, I plodded around their edges, and came back to my little room with my tray of tubes and discovered what was killing them. Several times I was an enemy of the people, as in that play. Poor half-dead Loomis creek had a pig farmer to thank for its condition. I had to trace the infection up a side-creek. The farmer pointed a rifle at me and found himself in court.

'A pig himself,' Bets said.

'But I didn't give up on fungi. I always loved them best.' I showed her my two books on the subject.

'That's not a good cover,' she said, tapping it.

And that's a nasty dress you're wearing, I could have said.

Restrained myself because I was happy. It came from two sources equally: Alice at her work, a creature I am able to admire; and Neville at home, growing old and keeping young, and keeping Alice company.

I did not tell Bets about Neville. He's not for sharing. Neville is mine.

I returned to the Harvey with a sharp-cut profile and a lying full face. I tried to let nothing of my reduction show, but my work-mates knew more about me on some levels than I did. They knew when to pat me with a cheerful word and when to step away to some just-remembered task on the other side of the room. Doctor Staines would have liked to get rid of me but could find no excuse. I lifted myself into each day – made up in a week or two the six weeks I'd had off – and kept my work moving, its focus exact. Professionally I was sharp and hard. What I had to manage outside the Harvey was to step this plain person out of the mirror and turn her into me again.

There was no large way of doing it. When I came home I sank into apathy. Yet food had to be cooked, clothes washed, my body washed. I managed it, and each task – clipping my nails, brushing my hair – raised me a tiny step towards my former self. I sat in the living-room or at the kitchen table and went back through my working day, replaying each thing I'd done and word I'd said. It was like cells multiplying. As I grew, Richie Ayres shrank until he was no more than bothersome – sharply bothersome at times. I had to endure some years of having him fastened on me like a leech, but in the end I shook him off – 'Get out of my life' – and squashed him under my foot. There's a bloodstain on the carpet. Chemwash doesn't get it out . . . Enough of this. I'm playing a bit with Richie and that's part of the stain.

While this was going on – there's a huge 'meanwhile', a huge dark planet, circling my life – Father and Mother kept me informed about Gordon. His condition was similar to mine, except that as I worked my way back to my centre he went out to his edge, and somewhere beyond. Marlene's parents threatened him with the police if he did not stop pestering them. Marlene had shifted, they said. She did not want to see him any more. He left letters for her in their box, saying that he knew they were lying. He waylaid her friends until they grew frightened of him – and, of course, they had no idea where she was. 'Australia,' Marlene's father shouted from his front porch, 'and she's not coming back. Now get out of here. I'm phoning for the police.'

All this time she was in Christchurch living with an aunt. I don't know when her minders discovered she was pregnant. I don't know whether giving up the baby was her idea. My guess is that she was incapable of judgement by that time.

Australia. It had the ring of truth. Gordon had turned his life to searching for Marlene, and that huge country with its dry desert heart . . . I'm speculating. He wrote to Mother and Father, saying little more than: I'm in Sydney now, I'm in Brisbane, in Melbourne. They had a letter from as far away as Perth. I don't believe he was searching by that time. He was letting Marlene's loss – and something else, something else – settle in his heart and drain away the possibility of 'other people'.

He stopped writing after Perth. Guessing again, I say that someone in Wellington told him Marlene had killed herself. So he had nobody left. Marlene dead. Handy dead. His sister Alice lost and gone as surely as Marlene.

Although it probably did not matter where he lived after that, he made his way back to Wellington and began his life on the streets. He became a familiar figure, growing older, shabbier, more bent, remote from voices and gestures aimed at him. I've spoken with people who said that for several years he wore a suit but when it fell to pieces he took his clothes out of charity bins. Others say that he sometimes smiled and said hello. That must have been in the early days, in the sixties perhaps, when he told the president's men that he ate scones. Later on he kept his eyes down, seeing no more than the pavement, seeing shoes and whatever occupied his mind.

He wasn't known as Gordon. His name was Cyril.

And I knew none of this. When I thought of him I pictured Paddington, Kings Cross, the Harbour Bridge, Bondi Beach, with Gordon – how shall I put it? – sloping along, minding his business, and working quietly at finding his way back to us. For many years I believed he would come.

Lecturing at a conference in Sydney in 1974, I looked for his face in the audience. If I had seen him I would have rushed down from the podium. 'Gordon, Gordon,' I was ready to cry. That night I went out from my hotel in the central city and walked along Oxford Street, miles and miles, as far as Bondi Junction, and back on the other side, looking into restaurants and side streets, into buses passing by, and looking for tin shacks like his one in Ghuznee Street. Back at my hotel, I stepped into the warmth and quiet of the foyer, and knew that I must not do that sort of thing again. I telephoned Neville in Auckland – it was after midnight back there – and told him I had given up Gordon. I told him Gordon was wherever he was, doing whatever he did, and I'd leave him there, and Neville said: 'He's like a fish in the sea. Don't try and catch him any more. Think of porpoises, Alice. Or sprats if you like, with a silver flash. Think of him being where he belongs.' It was helpful advice, although without the magic he intended.

Meanwhile Gordon was in Wellington. Gordon was not Gordon any more.

Neville was Neville right to the end. He was the whole man in my life. All the others have bits dropping off, more each time I remember them; and I have to fit Richie together like Frankenstein's monster to understand his effect on me. There's a sense in which I'm a made thing too, in which my mental health is fictile. It's like a jar Neville turned on a wheel and shaped with his hands.

At one o'clock I sat on a bench in the Harvey grounds. Once again I had forgotten to cut my lunch. Neville came out and sat beside me. He rattled a brown paper bag under my nose.

'Sandwich?' he said.

I took one. 'God, Neville, they're awful,' I said.

'What's wrong?'

'Marmite on stale bread. I haven't had one of these for twenty years.'

'Good healthy tucker. Eat up.'

The Marmite burned my tongue and the bread scoured my mouth. I ate complaining.

He said: 'I've got a spare bedroom if you want. Nice big room. You could put in a desk. You might want to sew new curtains. I don't know.'

'I can't sew.'

'You can have the sunroom as a sitting-room. You wouldn't have to see much of me. I don't want your stockings drying in the bathroom though.'

'People would say I was your mistress,' I said.

'Do we give a brass razoo what people say?'

I was his lodger for a year, then his mistress – no, lover, I prefer that – then his wife. We slipped away one afternoon and married in the registry office, with a clerk as witness. I said we should go for a drink, then back to work, but Neville drove out of town instead and we walked the length of Rabbit Island beach, I with my stockings off and skirt tucked up and he with his trouser bottoms rolled. Each wave carried thousands of tiny tuatua up the sand. Their shells were almost transparent, half the size of my thumbnail. They poked out their tongues and burrowed in, were gone in a second, millions of tiny lives under the sand. Neville had known they would be coming ashore. It made a perfect wedding day. As for bridal white, my feet in the waves were washed as white as snow.

Our living together had been a scandal to some, and our marriage proved to others that I had not recovered my wits. We did not give a brass razoo or a tinker's cuss. I have never been more simply contented than with Neville. Contentment became my peak of happiness. To hell with ecstasy: it's over-rated; it's chocolate fudge. Makes you fat, then collapses your cells until your outside sags and your inside turns to sludge. Contentment with Neville kept me active, kept me lean. I had to run to keep up with him, then learn to sit quiet, holding hands, at the end of the day. I felt as if I owned all my bones, all the flesh on them and the blood in me, down to the busy capillaries in the ends of my toes. Mind and body were alive, both up and jumping; our love-making was friendly and good, and sleep a renewal for the day to come. The image our lives in Nelson conjours up is of a clinker-built dinghy with a skinny-shanked outboard motor puttering at the back. It noses into reeds and the shingly mouths of creeks, where Neville and I nearly tip out in our eagerness to uncover, to see. Then it lifts its snout and speeds to the opposite shore – the old motor beating the water like eggs – where we sit on a pebble beach, beside a driftwood fire, and talk over what we have found. Neville and I: unglamorous, busy, secure. We were well matched.

He was vain about the number of names he could call himself: soil chemist, zoologist, lepidopterist, and more. The one he was proudest of was coleopterist, and among the coleoptera, weevils were the ones he liked best. Their long noses, made for pushing in, appealed to him. Once or twice we collaborated, most notably on beetles that carry fungal spores, but his important work had been done years before – on pine weevils (the timber industry has cause to thank him) and an Australian termite that attacked telegraph poles and wharf piles. What else? The flax-infesting weevil, the gorse seed weevil, Fuller's rose weevil, the apple seed chalcidoid wasp, codling moth, the wheat-sheath miner, parasites for slaters and earwigs – all these in his work for the Harvey and the DSIR, while at home, in his back garden, in his kumara bed, he carried out experiments on the breeding habits of the yellow admiral butterfly. Inside, in every space, he kept his collection of shells, one of the largest in New Zealand (Neville as taxonomic conchologist was unrivalled). In a workroom off the kitchen he mounted specimens of whatever walked or flew or swam. When I moved in he was scraping frog bones and wiring them into skeletons, using a twist drill he had made from a darning needle flattened at the point and bevelled on the edges.

In Auckland he took up what he called his new position – free spirit – although I told him he had been that all his life. When I went out on fieldwork he came as my unpaid assistant, although our positions often seemed reversed. He knew as much about fungi and algae as I in the end.

This scrawny, leathery, slightly mad old man. His eyes of brightest blue. His mind that probed like a weevil's snout. Good science, he told me once, brought the imagination into agreement with reality – a long journey most of the time, and one that both refined and intoxicated. At secondary school our English teacher read us a poem – I don't remember the title or the author – that had a man in it who had fed on honeydew. I have seen Neville do that many times, standing by a black beech tree, sipping translucent droplets with the tip of his tongue, then turning with 'flashing eyes and floating hair' (another bit from the poem) to beat off wasps competing for them. I tasted honeydew once or twice, but did not make a habit of it because it was excreta from scale insects under the bark. Neville said excreta was just a word, and anyway, no matter what end it came out of, sweetness was a gift from God (in whom, by the way, he did not believe). 'Weave a circle round him thrice and close your eyes with holy dread' – another bit. I never did that. He invited me inside and I went happily, and count my years with him the best of my life.

We bought a house on the Scenic Drive, along from Titirangi. Auckland lay spread out at our feet. My mother and father lived down there in a weatherboard bungalow overlooking a mangrove creek. We dropped down the hill road like a stone into a puddle. Loomis, a suburb now, lay off to the west. We bypassed New Lynn, where years before our family had driven to the flicks at the Delta, Pt Chevalier where the loonies had been kept, and the zoo where animals less dangerous than mad people had paced and glared in their cages, and came to Meola creek and Earl and Merry Ferry. Their only way of coping with Neville was by good manners. They retreated into cups of tea and slices of fruit cake. He signalled me, spiking up his hair, when he couldn't take any more, and I said: 'Neville wants to have a look at the mangroves,' and he said: 'See if I can find any crocodiles,' and Mother always said, when he was gone: 'Are you sure you're all right, Alice?' I told them I was, and did not ask if they were. They would have said yes, and believed it too, although Father was still practising his vice. He was husband to Mother and gardener to Mrs Imrie, now Mrs Weeks, 'helping her out'. Trevor Weeks trained horses at the Avondale racecourse. Although he came home to eat and sleep, he had left Mrs Imrie – I can't help calling her that – years before. He worked his horses in the morning and spent his afternoons in the pub, and in a number of what his wife called 'widowy beds'. His horses ran last almost as if he trained them for it, yet a string of one-horse owners kept his stables full: failed bookies, suburban grocers, factory storemen, mates who had been brickies all their lives and had always dreamed of owning a horse. (That pair shifted their gelding and won a race, Father showed me in the *Herald* – how they grinned!)

Weeks treated Mrs Imrie badly. She had bruises to powder, all over again. Father grew moist-eyed at her plight. Every two or three weeks he loaded his mower and clippers in the boot of his car and drove out to Avondale to tidy her section. 'Trimming her edges,' Mother said drily when I stopped by. There was no stress, no jealousy, in my parents' house; they had reached a marvellous understanding. He would never leave her, he loved her best, while she wanted only to be unfussed and have his company when she needed it. To maintain her position she allowed him to 'exercise his compassion', as Neville put it. I wanted to know if Mrs Imrie still wore a housecoat and mules.

I did not look in my letterbox for a letter from Gordon, but when I visited Mother and Father could not prevent myself from feeling in theirs before going inside. At some point Mother would say: 'Have you heard from Gordon?' – say it casually, as though letters from him were a regular event. When I said no, Father would nod his head and say in a voice pitched a little higher than usual: 'He'll be in touch.'

'When he's ready,' Mother would say. They succeeded each other as though performing a litany.

I held myself as sharp as a blade, but lost my edge as the years went by, until I wondered what I would do if I spotted him somewhere. Rush forward and crush him in my arms? Watch from behind a potted fern? Sneak away? I tried various figures and formulae to explain our condition, his and mine: we were two particles affecting each other in a quantum way – action at a distance, it is called. That helped for a while; but I needed to know where he was and what speed he was travelling and whether he was particle or wave. It's a conceit that lost its efficacy as it grew old. Then I thought of myself as a cracked tooth that did not affect my biting and chewing, but now and then some cold or hot thing, Gordon, touched the nerve . . . I'm only reminded of it because I have a tooth like that now. Neville's sprat flashing in the sea was, as I have said, useful for a while. I changed the sprat to a salmon to give it weight.

Gordon never got in touch. My parents died without hearing from him. The same will happen to me, but I know why.

Mother went first: a mini-explosion in her brain. How lucky she was. Father took longer and suffered more. I tried to get Mrs Imrie – a widow by that time, with a surprising amount of money that sly Weeks had salted away – to lend a hand in caring for him, but she told me she was no good at that sort of thing. 'I'll pop in and see him now and then. Does he like chocolates? You know, in all these years I've never found out.' She came once, sat for twenty minutes with her painted fingernails pricking the back of his hand, and I didn't see her again until the funeral.

I'm shuffling twenty years like playing cards. Work and home and family, illness and growing old, deception, remorse, forgetfulness – I lay them down, but always play Neville as my trump card. He became frail, his joints malfunctioned, his eyes began to darken, but he never once blamed his body or saw it as other than himself. His skin was his boundary. Mind, he insisted, went that far. Poor circulation was a kind of forgetting. He sent his mind down to his frozen feet to find out what was going on. Liver marks on his hands? He found out why. Aging became his study and, in a way, his entertainment. 'See –' he would show me, sliding and compressing the skin on the backs of his hands – 'I can make new territory. Ridges and gullies and mountain ranges. It's terra incognita, love. We could set out to conquer the West. And watch if I push the other way. A different land. You could hide from a posse doing that. Slip into a different universe.'

He had to stop fine work because of his eyes. One night, just before his pancreatic cancer was diagnosed, a car in front of ours on the Scenic Drive knocked over a possum. I got out and carried the body to Neville. He felt its bones all over and found them unbroken, so we took it home. The next day he skinned and gutted it, then spent several days scraping its bones. He dried and articulated them, then wired and glued them in a crouching position. It was his last piece of work. When I left Auckland I gave the skeleton to a school. His other things – shells and all – went to a museum.

He was moderately friendly to his cancer but never granted it more than outsider status. He called it the lodger. It killed him in only four months. His doctor found secondaries, and several days later Neville whispered to me: 'The lodger has taken over the house so I'm moving out of doors.' He died soon afterwards, midway between Mother and Father.

I had looked for Gordon at Mother's funeral. I did not look for him at Neville's. He had no place.

Now the card with Father's face on it. He was a robust old man, although weak in his mind. I wanted him to die mowing Mrs Imrie's lawn. That would have been appropriate. But he too went from cancer, and I won't go into it. It took longer than Neville's and wasted him from twelve stone to six, from a man with a big, kindly visage to a huge-eyed monkey or spectre-faced lemur – with, thank God, its understanding drugged. I sat with him as he died quietly.

I wanted Gordon at Father's funeral. I looked for him in the crematorium chapel and later outside on the paths, thinking perhaps I might see him striding away. I would not have run after him, but I fantasised that he would turn and wave before going on among the graves. But only Mrs Imrie was there, on a wooden bench, smoking a cigarette in a holder. I said goodbye to the half dozen people who had come, and sat with her.

'I didn't come inside, dear, because I would have cried and there's nowhere to fix my make-up.'

She told me Father had been a sweetie, her favourite man, then changed it to second favourite. The thing that was wrong with him was he had no oomph. I did not go into that, but asked about the man waiting in her car. He looked like a bruiser. Mrs Imrie would score some more black eyes.

'Oh,' she said, 'someone to keep me company. Don't stay too long a widow, Alice. Although, come to think of it, some of them . . .'

We chatted about Loomis, leaving out her second-favourite man. Imrie had married two more wives: got rid of the first – adultery again – then found himself ruled by the second. You saw them at the races, Mrs Imrie said, with Jock always half a step behind. The wife held out her hand without looking and he put whatever she needed into it. 'I smile at him but I don't think he knows who I am. Or really who he is any more. Poor Jock.'

The fat-necked man in the car flicked ash out the window. I looked at Mrs Imrie's crinkled chest and strawberry mouth. He was thirty years younger, and I might have found a way of warning her if I had not remembered Neville and me. Not that one could compare – yet she had bright eyes and a youthful readiness.

She said: 'I always liked your little brother. He was nice.'

'You knew him?' I said.

'Oh yes. Walking with his schoolbag. He helped me once when I broke the heel off my shoe. He walked me home. I had my arm right round a pretty boy. I think he got a wee bit excited. I might have asked him in if he'd been older.'

'I wish you had.'

'Other times – I mean with other boys . . . But I mustn't be naughty. That's why I was so upset when I saw him.'

'Who? My brother?'

'Didn't Earl tell you? He said he would. But I wasn't quite sure he understood.'

'You saw Gordon?'

'Oh yes, I saw him.'

So my brother came to me through the graves, as if, now that Father was dead, he could show himself. I felt his presence behind me and swung my head wildly to see; and he was not there – was lodged somehow in Mrs Imrie, who grew afraid as I demanded when and where, my hand biting her forearm, my questions striking hot clenched punches at her face. The bruiser in the car called out: 'You all right over there?'

'Yes, Roland, I'll call you,' Mrs Imrie said. 'Alice dear, it was him, I'm not gaga, you know. I'm good with faces. But he was – Alice, I told Earl – he was a tramp. His clothes were all filthy, there's no other word. And he looked about a hundred and five. Earl probably didn't hear me properly. Poor Earl, he was sick, and of course I never saw him again. But really, Alice, he was a sight – your brother, I mean. He was wearing a sort of filthy woollen cap and whiskers all over his chin. And he had this bucket with things in it . . .'

'Where? Where was he?'

'In Lambton Quay. The main street. And when I asked my friend she said: "It's one of the street people. He's called Cyril." But I knew who it was. I didn't follow him or say hello. My friend said he never talks to anyone or even meets their eye. Not that I would have, of course, because – how do I say it, Alice? – he had this smell . . .' She beckoned her boyfriend.

'How long ago? Now he'll be gone.'

'No, Alice,' she said, putting out her hands to have him pull her to her feet. 'She said he's been there for years and years and years. She said he's famous. Do you want to come for a drink, dear? You look as if you could use one.'

'No,' I said, 'I've got to hurry,' and I started for my car and beat Roland out the gate. I drove home deaf and blind (there's a phantom driver takes control), but after Pleasant Road and the hill to Titirangi began to understand I had no home any more, and for the rest of my drive, and walking up the path and opening my door and lying down on my wide double bed, I pulled and bullied Neville to my side and worked to have him displace Gordon there. He gave the sort of smile I had rarely seen, denying me, and in spite of my calling his name receded into the small, still place I've been able to visit since that time only when everything else is put away. I lost my name, widow, and shrank to sister, and heard myself wail with diminishment. Neville left with a silver flash. Gordon, in his many shapes, usurped his place – Gordon the child, Gordon walking on the sculpted paths, Gordon turning into Ghuznee Street on that night . . .

I lay on the bed with my brother for an hour. Then I stood up in the empty house and phoned for an airline booking and prepared my clothes – and my self – for Wellington.

There are growing pains. There are shrinking pains too.

Perhaps having piercings makes one sharp. Bets, for all her broad-ness of face, cuts like a knife. She was wearing a bushman's singlet today, her large breasts unrestrained inside, and a wrap-around skirt and sandals held together with rivets of industrial size. Her get-ups, her plain-ness, lead me to mistake her for dull, but I need only five minutes of her company to become aware of her clever brain shredding into finer bits everything I say.

'Why shift to Wellington if you worked in Auckland and Nelson all your life?'

'Not all,' I said. 'I was three years in England.'

She marked that down as evasion.

'Most people want to retire in Nelson. I would have thought you'd go there.'

'It's a nice place but I like something bigger.'

'Auckland's bigger.'

'Too big.'

She's like a woman with a basin of eggs, suspicious that one of them isn't fresh. I pretend we're making small talk, but hear the hesitation in my voice, so move from evasion to attack.

'What a nosy girl you are. I mean, you're from Napier and you've come here. What's your reason?'

'Mind your business,' she said.

'You mind yours.'

'Adrian came to find his grandfather.'

'And do my course,' Adrian said. He was uncomfortable at our bickering.

'You can't have had many friends here,' Bets went on, ignoring him.

'I've never needed friends. Well, one or two. The rest are clutter.'

'Wellington,' she said. 'Stuck up here on a hill. You're all alone, Alice. You must have known lots of people in Auckland.'

'I came because it's where my brother died.'

'Yeah, Bets, cool it, eh,' Adrian said. 'Hey, Alice, I'll take the car if that's OK. We want to have a look in the One Eye Gallery up in Paekakariki.'

'It needs petrol,' I said, looking at Bets.

'We'll put some in,' she said.

They drove away and left me trembling. The woman has sniffed out something false in me, but has no knowledge of the huge complexity of the simple thing she might uncover, as round and shining as a pearl. She'll make a mess. She wants a mess. She'll never believe I'm acting out of love.

After they left I took a bus downtown, hoping to see Gordon passing by, but Saturday is not one of his days. There are rooms where he sits in a corner, drinking tea, and I don't intrude. They're part of his weekend beat. I know mainly Molesworth Street and Lambton Quay, which I think of as a groove he follows. I keep in the groove, making my behaviour natural – a neat lady in a trouser suit and plain shoes, walking behind him and passing with a glance, or sitting on a seat as the world walks by. Here is Gordon. He is watchable. I watch. My conversations with him make no change in my face.

It was different when I first came to Wellington – but no, I won't go into that.

Adrian and Bets have not come back. I worry about the traffic on the dangerous strip of road into Paekakariki. But I suppose they've gone to her place, where they'll make love. A gallery in their day, then food and coffee, music, sex. I walked on the wharf for my treat, enjoyed the spring sunshine – the sun makes love to me – and the sea. As always when I'm happy, I was able to find Neville. It's easier now than it was when he first went away. I made room for him and we sat beside the harbour with our shoulders touching and his hand over mine. For a warm hour there were just the two of us. Then I stood up and said goodbye and took the bus across the crooked hill and through the tight cutting into Wadestown.

It's a calm night. Down in the city Gordon sleeps on a narrow bed. Or perhaps, because it's warm, he has walked to his shelter on the other side of the hill and lies with his hands crossed on his chest while the pine trees whisper overhead.

I imagine Marlene keeping him company. He finds his resting place in her.

SEVEN

Three weeks have passed since I wrote in this book.

Now our troubles start. I'm confused by love and resentment: love for Gordon and Adrian, the former pure but marked with a stain, the latter careful (that's care-full) and auntie-ish, although penetrated with intensity. My resentment is for the clever, pushy woman who has brought us – Gordon, me, Adrian – to this. I've got the feeling that she and Adrian are long term. She's not overheated, as I was with my young lover, Richie Ayres. She *cares* for him, which almost makes me care for her. But see what she has done with her interfering.

I am paralysed by fear.

I wrote that when I woke in the night. Now, in the morning, I am even more afraid. Adrian helped me to bed, then drove to what I suppose is now his home – Bets' flat in Berhampore, shared with two fellow art students. Yesterday we dropped her there. I told her I wanted to talk to Adrian alone. What I had to say was none of her business. Then I fired a parting shot: 'That skeleton isn't a cat, it's a possum. Which rather spoils the whole thing, don't you think?' Her broad cheeks blushed like the halves of a Doris plum.

The place, the paintings, seem implicated. I had not known the building existed or that such mad abundant making went on. It's an exhibition of student work held at Erskine College, a nunnery and girls' school formerly, at Island Bay. The Learning Connexion uses the building – and what a place, four storeys of workrooms and studios with high ceilings and creaking floors, linked by echoing staircases and half-lit corridors. Adrian drove me down the long road, and in the building Bets became our self-appointed guide. She maintained a cool proprietorial air, clipping her explanations short and watching for incomprehension with submerged belligerence. I grew dizzy turning into rooms, turning out – with image, colour, shape, with awfulness and excellence. There's probably no better way than one of these exhibitions for putting human diversity on show. Such an abundance of places in the mind and ways of seeing. Such mad self-belief and stupidity, with beauty emerging here and there, and courage, delight and despair. My susceptibilities were churned up. By the time we reached the top floor I was seasick.

Bets' installation was in an end room. She turned her back while I looked at it – more likely from strong-mindedness than cowardice. We circled the thing, Adrian and I, in different directions, and I saw from the keenness on his face as we passed that he 'got it' and was impressed. I got it too. 'Truth and Falsehood' was the name, and it was supposed to mean that nature is cruel but, by definition, natural, and man is unnatural by failure and design. Something like that. Bets had spread a tarpaulin on the floor and covered it, left to right, with sand, pebbles, artificial grass and slabs of asphalt. The asphalt was the human end. A little cardboard city of skyscrapers stood on it. Toy trucks and petrol tankers travelled along roads drawn with chalk. Toy warplanes waited on runways. The proportions were wrong but Bets wasn't worried by that. On the grass plastic cows grazed in geometrical paddocks. Plastic trees grew in straight lines, dwarfed by a set of false teeth and a Steinlager can. There was also a condom, which seemed to have been used. Natural things appeared where the grass and pebbles met: driftwood, feathers, a fern frond, a weta, a paua shell. The sand was scattered with pipi and cockle shells, and a bare patch of tarpaulin at the end was painted in loops of blue for the sea. The cruelness and naturalness of nature were represented by the skeleton Bets took for a cat (in her defence, it was incomplete) lying on the sand with its claws embedded in what we at the Harvey used to call a flat rat.

I have to say my first thought was: Oh dear. It's my final thought too.

Adrian wrapped her in a bear hug. 'It's great, Bets,' he said.

She loosened his arms to see me over his shoulder, and I gave a smile I hoped would be taken for approval.

'So?' she said.

'It's quite a story,' I said.

She didn't like that.

'It's conceptual, Alice,' Adrian complained.

'But it spells everything out. And with that title too. I like the cat.'

'The title's a mistake,' Bets said. 'Anyway, let's leave it. Shall we go and sit in the car? There's something I want to say.'

I knew instantly that she'd found me out. Her face was refined by determination.

I said: 'I think I just want to go home. I'm not feeling well.'

'Alice?' Adrian said, peering at me. 'Yeah, you've gone white. Is there somewhere she can sit down, Bets?'

'I don't want to sit down. I want to go home.'

'What about a drink of water, eh? Can you get one, Bets?'

He helped me out of the room and along to the head of the stairs. I thought: I could fall down here and break my neck. That might be best.

Bets came out of a room full of wooden tubs, carrying a cup of water. I sipped it, although the cup was stained like old false teeth.

We went down flight by flight, with Adrian supporting me and Bets in front in case I should fall. The paintings I'd tried to take in went by in reverse order – red hills, savage crows, lovers, fish, motor cars, a wide-open cherry-red vagina. I'm in a madhouse, I thought, and Bets is going to tear me open. The ground floor steadied me. I got ready for stubbornness, for sewing my mouth shut.

Adrian helped me into the back seat of the car. I leaned back and closed my eyes, then felt the car settle as Bets and Adrian climbed in front.

'No,' she said, blocking him from inserting the key. 'Alice –' turning to me – 'I think you're only putting it on.'

'Hey, Bets,' Adrian said.

'Well, she is.'

'You stupid girl,' I said. 'It isn't some little squabble. I've been in this thing for forty years.'

'For Christ's sake, what's going on?' Adrian said.

'Start the car,' I said.

'No,' Bets said. 'It'll take ten seconds for what I've got to say.'

'Say it then. Say it. And whatever you think you've found out is wrong.'

'OK. I've been looking in the papers for 1962. No one got killed on a motorbike on Brooklyn hill.'

'No?'

'No. And another thing. The Brooklyn trams stopped running in 1957. So your brother didn't go under a tram.'

My eyes had, of course, come open. Bets and I were shooting at each other.

'You shouldn't have talked to her, Adrian,' I said.

'Just as well he did,' Bets said.

'I'm going home now. You can get out at your flat.'

'No way. We've got a few questions we need answers to.'

'We?' I said. 'Will you start the car, Adrian? Or I'll drive myself.'

'Is this true about the trams?' he said.

'Probably. I didn't have time to do research.'

'So what's it all about then?'

'I'll tell you when you've got rid of her. Now I'm not saying another word. In fact, I think I'll just lie down.'

Which I did, on the seat. It's uncomfortable, and a short way along the road to Berhampore I sat up again. Bets and Adrian were shooting each other now. He was saying it wasn't her business any more and she was insisting it was; she'd done all the work and she wasn't giving up until she knew. I thought: This will break them up – or else they'll come back together with flashing lights. I did not care which. Gordon, I thought, I won't let them hurt you, I promise you that.

As Bets got out I told her that her cat was really a possum.

'You getting in the front?' Adrian said.

'No, I'll stay here. And don't ask, Adrian. Not until I've had a cup of tea.'

He drove home, remarkably self-controlled. Didn't say a word, even when I felt compelled to say: 'I really like Bets. Please don't think I don't.'

In the house I asked him to put the kettle on. 'I'm not going to feel like dinner tonight, so if you're eating here you'd better order a pizza.'

'I'm not eating here.'

'Do you mean ever again?'

'That depends. Is he alive?'

'Yes, he's alive.'

I went into the sitting-room and took my chair looking over

the harbour. Yachts with pumped-up sails competed in a race. Everybody wanted to win. Wanting to win is one of the things that drives Bets along. But, of course, there's more to her. Perhaps it's curiosity. Perhaps it's love. Meanwhile, Gordon ... There is nothing to say. He compels silence.

Adrian brought me a cup of tea. He must have been thinking while the kettle boiled, and the magnitude of my lie had bullied him away from his desire to know into a perception of me, the run of my life over the forty years I had flung at Bets. He looked at me as though I was ill and steadied the cup and saucer in my hands.

'You all right now?'

'Yes, Adrian, there's nothing wrong with me. But I want to be quiet while I drink this.'

He sat down, and after a moment said: 'I thought it was a possum too.'

'It doesn't necessarily spoil it,' I said.

We were quiet again. I finished drinking and put my cup on the coffee table. The yachts had gone from sight, except for a slow one with a yellow sail shaped like a pear.

'I don't suppose he had a motorbike,' Adrian said.

'Yes he did. But it didn't go. He was going to fix it up and take Marlene for rides.'

'So where is he now?'

The question brought enormous relief to me, and a flush of pleasure so intense I almost fainted. At last someone was sharing Gordon with me. But dread sounded too, like a nail scratching on tin.

'Can I just tell you some things and ask you not to say anything?'

'Yeah, all right. But Jesus, you've been stringing me along for the last bloody year. What is he? Some big lawyer, some fat accountant? Is he going to be ashamed of me?'

'No,' I said, 'it's nothing like that.'

'I'm finding him for my father. I'll just tell him Dad's name and say goodbye.'

'You won't tell him anything.'

'Why not? Why the mystery? Why all these fucking lies, Alice?'

'Don't swear at me.' I'm offended by some of the words people use today. The 'f' one – which I used once to my father – is by no means the worst. They pick them up from American movies. I'm no prude. I hate the feebleness more than the ugliness – I mean the impoverishment – and it pains me when I hear someone I love sliding down there, even when he's moved by strong feelings. I said: 'I want you to sit still and hear what I'm going to say. Then you can say "damn it" if you like' – trying to help him with a joke – 'but I'm not taking questions, Adrian. Not tonight. There are reasons for everything I've done and you'll learn them when the time is right.'

He told me to get on with it.

'Gordon lives here in Wellington. He's not Gordon any more, he's changed his name.'

'Why? What to?'

'That's a question. I said none.'

'So where does he live? What does he do?'

I shook my head.

'Is he married? Got kids? All of that?'

'Adrian, I won't answer. Soon I'll let you find out for yourself. All I'm doing now is – motorbikes and trams. Are you going to listen?'

'You told me about changing his name.'

'Yes, that much. Now I'm going back. He worked at the hospital and lived in the bach in Ghuznee Street. Marlene was his girlfriend. You know all that. What you don't know is – in 1959 a man was found dead in his front yard. He'd been stabbed.'

'Who?'

'An old alcoholic. A street person. Gordon used to make friends with them and give them money. This dead man was one of them.'

'Who did it?'

I closed my eyes and shook my head. 'No one knows. They never caught anyone. But the thing is, Marlene was the one who found the body. Gordon used to leave a key for her in a pile of bricks. She was getting it out when she saw the body lying by the wall. She'd been ill, Adrian. You know about the psychiatric ward. It was where Gordon met her. When she saw this body lying there she – flipped.' I made a sound of disgust at the stupid word. 'She ran away and people found her in the street with blood on her. So, for a while, the police thought she'd done it.'

'Who did? Was it Gordon? He's been in prison, is that what you're saying?'

'No, no, no. I told you, they never caught the person. Gordon was at work. He was working late. And they soon found out it wasn't Marlene. But her family grabbed her, they wouldn't let Gordon see her. They took her down to Christchurch. That's where your father was born. You know all this. The baby was adopted. After that Marlene killed herself.'

'Jesus. Jesus.' Lost for words.

I said: 'Pour me a little sherry, Adrian. Have one yourself.'

When he didn't move I got up and did it myself – not little ones either.

The harbour was empty, the last yacht gone under the hill. The sea was white, but it darkened as I watched. Light from the setting sun flashed from the windows of houses in the bush above Day's Bay.

'Gordon was gone by that time,' I said. 'They told him Marlene was in Australia so he went there.'

'How do you know all this?'

'My parents came down. They tried to help him. They told me what was happening.'

'I would have thought you'd come across. For your brother.' He kept it to only a small sneer.

'I had troubles of my own,' I said.

I told him Gordon had written letters – short letters, postcards sometimes – telling them which part of Australia he was in. Then they stopped. For more than thirty years no one in the family knew where he was. Our parents died without knowing.

'I don't know when he came back. But he's been here in Wellington most of the time.'

'When did you find out?'

'The year my father died. 1991. So I came down and saw him –' choosing my words carefully – 'and found out where he'd been all that time, and when I retired from my job I shifted permanently. To be near him. I bought this house.'

He was watching me. I sipped my sherry. He hadn't touched his.

'Yeah?' he said.

'Yes. It's a good house. Neville would have been happy here.'

'So what's the thing you're not telling me?'

'Oh,' I said, and sipped again, 'I'm telling you nothing at all. You've been a good boy. You've been kind to me. And I know you were good to your father. But I don't actually have to *tell* you anything. I'm almost persuaded to let you see for yourself.'

'See Gordon?'

'Yes, see him. But you'd have to promise not to speak to him.'

Then I drew back. I was giving too much away. And I had *not* persuaded myself. Yet I could feel a kind of blind necessity at work, and hear a voice saying: End it. Whose voice? It hung between us like love, and I thought: I've got to do it, but I don't know whether it's for them or against.

I said: 'I think I can eat something after all. Will you go and order a pizza? You know the sort I like.'

'Are you saying he's gone gaga or something? Is he sick?'

'Will you do what I say.'

'Why all the guff? Motorbikes and trams? Why the fucking lie?'

'Please, Adrian. I'm going to cry.'

It wasn't for long. I dried my cheeks and finished my sherry, then started on his. He came back from the kitchen with a can of beer and sat nursing it and sulking for a while. Two sherries on an empty stomach made me light-headed. I kept on thinking: I've done it now, and felt fear and relief in equal parts. Another sherry would have made me sentimental, and I might have started thinking that Adrian would say some magic word and Gordon's lost years would fall away, and I would stand forgiven at his side . . .

Adrian said: 'I'm going to tell Bets.'

'If you have to.'

'I know you don't like her, but she's the best girl I've ever had. She's sensible.'

'That's because she's not a girl, she's a grown-up woman.' Except for her installations, I might have added. 'Do you mean she'll tell you what to do?'

We might have quarrelled, but the pizza man arrived. We ate in the sitting-room, off our knees. For something to say, I told him pizzas hadn't existed when I was a girl, or Kentucky Fried Chicken or Big Macs or Coca Cola, all the things that had been there for all of his life. And fries were chips, and chips were better. And you could buy oysters for one and six a dozen.

He said: 'Don't start.'

'Crayfish too. Crayfish were cheap. Gordon wouldn't eat them when he found out you boiled them alive.'

'Gordon was a wuss.'

I asked him to explain the word, then agreed that Gordon had some of that, but he was more, much more, more, more more...

'That's three sherries, Alice. You'd better slow down.'

He made mugs of tea and sat keeping me company late into the night. I kept dozing off and waking up and telling another story about Gordon: Brahn boots, I told that, and his drawing for the Boyles and, to show he wasn't really a wuss, his football injuries and winning at the inter-school athletic sports. I told him about our parents' marriage. Then went back to when Gordon was only eight and he played the part of the king in a play Standard Two put on at the Loomis School fancy dress party in the town hall. He sat at a table, wearing pyjamas, slippers, a dressing-gown and a cardboard crown pasted over with gold paper. He sorted florins and shillings into piles. 'The king was in his counting house counting out his money,' Gordon said. The queen wore a long dress and a silver crown. The maid wore an apron and a cardboard nose. The girl who was the blackbird had black wings. Why was Gordon in pyjamas and a dressing-gown? I don't know. He wore them not just for the play but right through the party; and told me on one of my trips to Wellington that he still had nightmares in which he found himself dressed in pyjamas in the street or on buses and trams, and sometimes he wore nothing at all.

'We all have those,' Adrian said.

'Do we?'

'Sure. Ask your shrink. You probably need one.'

'He said it was the worst night of his life, dressed in pyjamas.'

'What were you?'

'Maid Marian. Standard Three did a play too.'

I went to sleep in my chair and woke to hear him washing the dishes.

'Come on, Alice. Time you were in bed,' he said, coming back.

'I don't need help. You can take the car. I think I might give it to you.'

He looked startled. 'Tell me when you're sober.'

'If I'm drunk it's not with sherry. I need the bathroom.'

He helped me there. At the door, maudlin, I said: 'Be kind to her, Adrian. She's a good girl. But make sure she's kind to you too.'

'Shall I run a bath?'

'That would be nice. I think she's not quite as kind as she should be.'

'Shut up, Alice,' he said, in a friendly way.

I remember it all clearly, but don't remember the bath. I imagine he waited outside the door in case I drowned – drowning was a possibility. I'd slipped sideways from Gordon, helped by sherry – another glass with my pizza – into the kind of safety that produces tears and soft focus and no real knowledge or feeling at all.

Then I was in bed, afraid again, with the warm sort of fear that makes its own forgetfulness. He said, from a distance: 'Goodnight,' and the car – had I really given it to him? – made cat-purring noises and went away.

I slept as though fingers had pulled my eyelids down, and woke with a dry mouth and a headache in the small hours. There was nothing to soften my fear. 'I'm frightened,' I said, and turned on the light and drank the glass of water Adrian had left on the bedside table; then reached for my book and pencil from the drawer, and wrote: Now our troubles start . . .

It's afternoon. Yachts are racing again, on a blue harbour sprinkled with confetti. They are crowded together, dipping their sails at each other as though they don't care about competing today. I walked in my garden, seeking freshness, a while ago, but I'm stuffed with fur, with cotton wool, and can't seem to touch anything. I shouldn't have eaten that warmed-up pizza for lunch. I feel sick.

Did I really say all that last night?

I am paralysed by fear.

EIGHT

Gordon walked back to Marlene waiting on the footpath. I stopped a short way up the street and watched. He put his arm around her, perhaps for the first time in such an easy way, and she put both of hers around him and they went into the hall, Gordon upright, not looking back, and Marlene in the awkward way hugging women have, leaning into him, with her hip-bone in the way.

We passed out of each other's lives, or so it seemed.

More than thirty years later I walked behind him up Lambton Quay and Willis Street, past the building that had been the St George Hotel and over the Dixon Street intersection. He came to the traffic lights at Ghuznee Street. I'm not sure he knew how to signal for the green man, or that the exit road from The Terrace tunnel ran over the spot where his shack had stood and where Marlene had found Cyril Handy's body. He did not turn his head left or right but knew enough not to step into the traffic.

I had waited for him at the central part of Lambton Quay, opposite Kirkcaldies, where Mrs Imrie had seen him. It took me three afternoons. I ate a sandwich and drank take-away coffee in Midland Park, and poked around in shops, buying little things to ward off suspicion and keeping my eyes on the street. I stood on the footpath, then followed a beat, fifty metres up and fifty metres down, and if I had not been so plainly respectable might have been taken in for questioning. Would I have had the wit to say: 'Sometimes I eat scones'?

I don't know where Gordon had been that day – possibly to some place that dispensed cups of tea. (He did not sleep in his shelter on Tinakori Hill until summer had set in.) I was under the walkway roof at Midland Park, watching the opposite footpath and wondering whether it was time to go around social agencies and night shelters when I saw him beyond the cars and buses – saw an apparition with my brother inside. He walked on the edge of the pedestrian flow, slowly, head down, and I knew at once, by revelation flashing from the years we had been together, that he was not cast out but was where he had chosen to be. It was as if he had shifted half a second outside time, and was ahead of, or perhaps behind, the people passing – their heads turning, some towards him and some away – and that the fragment of time, Gordon's step aside, made an unbreakable wall between him and all that went on commonly: between him and me, Gordon and Alice. I came against a barrier at my sight of him, was stilled as though by a shouted order. I was full of recognition of all things – *all things* – about my brother. So I did not shriek his name and run at him through the traffic. I said, or groaned – a birthing groan – 'Oh. Oh,' so loudly that a man next to me stepped away. I crossed to the centre of the road to be closer, then waited for the pedestrian light and crossed the rest of the way. I followed Gordon, ten steps behind, up Lambton Quay and Willis Street.

I had no idea where he would lead me or where I was going in time – through the wall, into the place where Gordon lived? I said: I want to go with you, I don't want you to come with me. I knew I must not, must never, want that. Gordon would die.

When the green man appeared, Gordon crossed. I passed him

160

and waited on the other side. He wore sneakers with the laces taken out. They went flop flop as he walked. His trousers were made for a shorter man, showing rumpled socks and a hand's width of white shin. He wore two jackets, the inner one an ancient quilted vest with a broken zip, the outer cast off from a pinstriped suit. He, or someone else, had scissored off the sleeves below the elbow. Underneath was an orange and brown checked flannel shirt, the sort made in China. He carried a bundle tied with twine under his arm and a plastic bucket in his other hand. Inside were a new-looking thermos flask and a woollen hat.

I waited for him to look at me but he passed without a glance, his eyes on the footpath. His margin was ten feet, and feet were all he saw of other people. I quickened my step and passed again, said: 'Gordon,' as he approached, the way one says a child's name, calling him easily to table. He stopped, not at my voice, but because he could not move around me. My shoes, my knees, perhaps my waist, he saw.

'Thank you,' he said. It was a voice with everything taken out.

'It's Alice,' I said.

'Thank you.'

'Leave him alone,' a man passing said.

'Mind your business,' I said.

'You all right, Cyril?' he asked.

'Thank you,' Gordon said.

I stepped aside and he went on.

'He never talks, lady. You can't do him any good.'

'How would you know?'

I trailed behind my brother, held on a thread, and when he stopped at the crossing by the Bar Bodega, looped it in until we stood side by side.

'Hello, Cyril,' I said, hoping that giving him his chosen name would somehow lead him to 'Alice', but he replied only with a sinking of his head.

I thought: He's moved me out. He wouldn't know how to let me in if he wanted to. And I heard my voice agreeing, in acceptance and grief: Well, that's all right. I'm where I belong.

'Shall we cross?' I said.

Drizzle, hardly more than a mist, began to fall. It stood in tiny drops, like dust, in his eyebrows, which had bushed out in an elderly way. The middle part of his head was bald, with hair from the sides streaked over as though painted on.

I said: 'Why don't you put on your hat?' but then decided to say nothing more for fear that even his two-word response brought him closer to other people than he could go without feeling some sort of discomfort, even pain.

We went into a narrow street at the top of Cuba Street. I let him move ahead in the thickening rain. There must be a room in one of these houses, I thought, some dry place where he belongs, and someone who helps him with food and looks after him – surely some person he connects with.

The house he turned into was a two-storeyed villa with its fretwork and finials gone and veranda posts rotting. Oxalis and wild parsley grew in cracks in the asphalt yard. The front door was open. He went along a hallway into the gloom and turned into a room that the food smell identified as a kitchen.

A woman's voice said: 'Hello, Cyril. Had a nice walk?'

'Hello,' Gordon said.

'You'd better cook your chops tonight. They won't last another day,' she said.

By the front door, two steps in, I waited for his reply. Could he say more than Thank you and Hello?

'Put your thermos here, love. I'll give it a rinse,' the woman said.

'Thank you.'

Silence after that, except for kitchen steps, woman steps, on lino, a tap turning on and off, a cupboard closing. I walked along the hallway and looked into the room. Gordon was gone.

'Excuse me,' I said to the woman at the bench.

'Shit,' she said, putting her hand on her chest. 'You gave me a fright.'

'I'm sorry. I should have knocked' – taking her in: a swollen-ankled woman with a lopsided face, jaw pushed sideways, red-dyed hair springing in that direction too. My first thought was: an ex-tart. But not, I thought, someone Gordon had taken up with. The cupboards behind her had names in marker pen: Ted, Angus, Cyril, Ron . . . a dozen or more.

'Is this a boarding house?' I said.

'Yes,' she said. 'Ambrosia House, would you believe? I call it Fry-up House. Who are you?'

'I'm Alice Kite. The man who just came in . . .'

'What about him? What did he do?'

'Nothing,' I said. 'I followed him to see where he lived. I used to know him.'

'That would have been years ago,' the woman said.

'Where's he gone?'

'Up to his room. You won't see him out of there till tea time. How come you know Cyril?'

'I was –' I needed to sit down. 'May I?'

She frowned, then picked up my distress and angled a chair out from the table.

'Thank you.'

'Your hair's wet. Here.' She opened a drawer and gave me a tea towel. I wiped my face and hair. Then I did not know what to say, for it seemed that Gordon was returned to me whole, missing no parts, yet was utterly changed, missing everything. I knew his life, could pick it up and turn it around, yet I had no facts. He had come to this. I understood how. Yet what was 'this'? I felt that he had been gone from me all these years not from his own choice only but from my neglect, and now I reversed it, picked him up and held him tight – but could not see him, could not know. It was like the condition called blindsight, where your vision is knocked out on one side, yet another pathway allows you to put your hand on things you cannot see.

'It's time for my afternoon cuppa,' the woman said. 'Do you want one?'

'Please.'

She switched on a kettle and took two mugs from a cupboard without a name.

'My name's Sheena.'

'Mine's Alice. I'm . . .' I did not know what I was. 'Are you the owner here? Is it all men?'

'Huh. Unofficial manager, that's me. I do the cleaning. And yes, all men. If you can call them that. Ratbags, most of them. They'd shit in their own nests. Cyril's all right. He's the best. How come you know him? When was that?'

'The last time I saw him,' I said, 'was 1959.'

'I'm surprised you recognise him now. He's changed a bit.'

'Did you know him?'

'No. But they change. They're middle-aged one day and old men the next. I suppose they'd say the same about us.'

'How long has he been here?'

'Ever since I came. That's about, let's see, six years. He's had the same room all the time. It's up the top of the stairs and along at the end. If you put your arms out, you can touch both walls. Doesn't bother him. He won't shift anywhere else. What's your interest? You wouldn't have been his girlfriend, someone like you.'

'No, I just . . . knew him. Does he talk to you? Does he tell you anything?'

'Cyril doesn't say a word to anyone. Hello, Goodbye, Thank you, that's his lot.' She poured boiling water in the mugs. 'I've heard stories about him. Like, how he comes from Aussie and he's run away from his wife and kids, but I don't believe that.'

'Why not?'

'He's a gentle sort. He wouldn't do it. Here, love.' She handed me the tea towel again. 'Wipe your face.'

I held the towel to my eyes while she took the tea bags out of the mugs.

'Milk?' I heard her voice.

'Yes.'

'Sugar?'

'No.'

'I guess you knew him pretty well?'

'I used to,' I said. 'Not now.'

'Drink that. You'll feel better. It's not often anyone comes for one of them. Except social workers now and then. And the cops. We've had a couple of flashers, poor old sods. They're not the worst.'

'Cyril doesn't . . .?'

'No, not him. Like I said, he's a gentleman. It's just, his mind's gone. It's somewhere else. He's got it locked up. I'd like to know what's really in his head. But you can't see Cyril's eyes. He won't look in faces.'

'How does he pay?'

'His benefit. The owner's here every two weeks on the dot – gets it from them before they can booze it away. No rent, you're out.'

'Does Cyril drink?'

'Not now. They say he used to. He was on that island the Sallies used to run, so I've heard. He still goes to AA meetings though. Sits in the back. The other men say it's for the tea.' The woman laughed. 'He's addicted to tea. Did you see his thermos flask? He's worked through three or four of those. I fill it up for him before he goes out. Lots of sugar. He likes that. Are you sure you want to know all this, dear?'

'Yes,' I whispered. 'I want to know. What about food?'

'They cook for themselves. Although some of them just do pies and fish and chips and stuff. We've got one eats out of rubbish tins. That's Ted. But Cyril cooks. It's chops or sausages most of the time. He can fry. He's got a fry pan and a pot. He boils potatoes. He puts a bit of cabbage in on top.' She got up and opened the cupboard named Cyril. 'That's his stuff. Knife and fork. Thermos flask. Cup and plate. That's his bottle of sauce. He likes sauce.'

'What does he do? I mean, all day?'

'He sits in his room. That's in the morning. He goes out in the afternoon, with his bucket and his flask. He goes round a few places he knows and someone there tops up whatever he's drunk, and maybe they give him a sandwich and a plate of soup. Then he comes back and sits in his room until it's time to cook his bit of veggies and meat.'

'But in his room? He – what?'

'Told you, he sits. There's a bed in there and a chair. He sits. Or he lies down.'

'Is there a radio? Does he listen?'

'No radio. We don't have TV either. The owner doesn't run an airport lounge, he says. They've got their rooms. They take their food back there and eat, and then they bring their dishes down. Wash their own dishes. They know where the tea towels are. And the soap.' She looked at me sharply. 'I suppose if you got close enough you noticed he smells. That's not Cyril, that's his clothes. He's quite clean. He shaves when I tell him. He washes a bit, but there's parts he doesn't get to. I say to him, "It's time for a bath, Cyril," and he has one. I tell him, "It's time you washed your underpants. And your singlet and your socks. You better put your shirt in too." So he goes out in the wash-house and does it. He wears his pants and jacket while his shirt and stuff are drying. He gets by. You shouldn't feel sorry for Cyril.'

I said: 'I don't.'

I felt wrapped around him like a blanket. My mind was clear, avid to know more – and later on would know what to make of it all. Yet my body told me how things were. Tears still ran on my cheeks. I could not make my hand reach out to my mug of tea.

'Can I see his room?'

'That's a private place – that's what I reckon. Without him saying yes, and he can never say that. It's tiny, I told you. They all are. A bed and a chair, that's their lot. There's a window he can open if he wants to get on the fire escape. There'll be a fire here one day, that's my pick. The way they smoke.'

'Does he?'

'Cyril doesn't do anything.'

'If I tried to take him away . . .?' – although I knew I would not.

'You couldn't. He won't shift. He's going to die here. Or up in the bush. He's got a possie on Tinakori Hill. He sleeps there most times in the summer, gets water in his bucket from the tap in Grant Road, by the steps. He's got a little thermette for his tea. When you see him with his quilt he's sleeping there. But he pays his rent and comes back here whenever he wants. It's his room. The owner tries to put someone in – double up, the miserable sod. But I don't let him. It's Cyril's place. Why would you want to, anyway?'

'What?'

167

'Take him away?' She looked at me, brown eyes sharp with interest. 'You're not his wife?'

I drew a deep breath and pulled words out like bits of paper tied on a string: 'I'm his sister.' My body, not my mind, knew the import, releasing a squirt of urine into my pants.

'Thought it might be something like that,' Sheena said.

'And I haven't seen him for so long . . . and here he is . . .'

'Does he know you? No, course not. How long?'

'Thirty years. Thirty-two years.'

'Well, he wouldn't. Cyril doesn't know anyone, not like that. His mind's gone. I don't know whether from alcohol or something else. Maybe both. You'd know.'

'Yes, I know. And he's . . .'

'What?'

'Up there, on his bed?'

'That's what he does. You can decide, if you're next of kin, but I'd leave him there.'

'Yes,' I said, 'I will.' I knew I must.

'I wouldn't even try talking to him. Because there's a kind of balance and if you put that out he could go right away. I'm no expert. That's what I think.'

I had at least the central part of myself in command even though, around it, bits flew off, bits fastened on. I said: 'Is there some way I can pay for him?'

'His benefit does it. If you like . . .'

'Yes, what?'

'You can leave some money with me. I'll get him stuff. I'll leave it in his cupboard: he won't know where it's from – things are just there or not there. I'll get Snickers, he likes those. And fresh bread sometimes, and butter if you like. New underpants too. It's not my job . . .'

'I can pay you something.'

'Yeah, all right. What do you say? Thirty dollars a week – is that too much? Half for my time and extra work, and half for him. I'll get him a new pillow, he needs that.'

'Yes, thank you, thank you.'

'You can put it in an envelope and post it here. Sheena Gourlay is me.'

I took money from my purse and put it on the table. I wrote her name on a piece of paper. Then I went away, left Gordon lying on his bed, and I've never been back inside that house, although I've been as far as the gate many times, walking after Gordon. I haven't met Sheena Gourlay again, or seen more than the back of her, sweeping the porch. I sent her thirty dollars a week until she wrote that it was getting pinched. She gave me a bank account number and I do it by automatic transfer now – forty dollars, she put it up. I don't know how she uses it, but I trust her. I've seen Snickers bars in Gordon's bucket. I've seen him with a brand-new bucket – now grown old.

I pray – I sometimes beg – that she won't change jobs or die; that she'll see us out, Gordon and me.

I came down to Wellington two or three times a year until I retired. Then I bought my house in Wadestown, on the eastern buttress of the hill. In summer Gordon sleeps in his possie on the southern side, while I sleep in mine. I talk to him before I close my eyes: Stay warm and dry. The southerly is a winter wind, bringing icy rain. He's safe in Fry-up House in that season. I can't get the name out of my head, or the picture of Gordon frying chops at the stove. Yet I'm preserved from too much pain and guilt by stoicism. I'm stoical about what has happened to him and me. This is how our lives turned out. I see his progress through the town with his bucket, with his quilt, with his head forward like a turtle and his eyes fixed on the pavement – see it as Gordon responding to me.

At other times I want to turn up my head and scream. He can't bear to look at human faces. I did that. I want him once, only once, to raise his eyes and look at me.

Over these ten years I've talked to people – street people, vagrants, alcoholics, Salvation Army workers, women who run soup kitchens and night shelters and give out used clothing, and none of them know him well. 'You can't know Cyril,' the women say. All the same, they know stories about him: Cyril and the president's men. He had not long turned up in Wellington (Cyril is an Aussie to some of them) and in those days he was drinking. A while after that he went to the island for the cure and tea became his drink. Doesn't that show he had an idea of himself; doesn't it show his mind was all right? If he could stop and never drink again? They're not sure. He was always far away; he was gone, they say. They'd sooner tell stories, like the one about giving Gordon a pair of winter socks, which he would accept only one of because only one from his old pair had a hole.

When I say 'Gordon' they look at me strangely. I change to Cyril, which has always been his name for those who help him. He must have changed it, perhaps by deed poll, soon after Handy's death. Sheena Gourlay is the only one I've told I'm his sister. Others suspect a connection, but some think I'm a Wadestown lady coming close to sniff at poverty. I leave bits of money in envelopes and go away.

Gordon has grown twenty years older in ten years. His wrists are thinner and his hands have deep clefts between the metacarpal bones. His ears seem bigger but that's because his face has shrunk. I never see into it because of the tilt of his head. The vertebrae at the base of his neck stand out like seed potatoes. And his mouth, when I glimpse it . . .

Sheena Gourlay telephoned me: 'You won't see Cyril for a while. He's lost some teeth.'

I asked what had happened and she told me the man called Angus had hit him in the mouth with a bottle, for no reason at all. Then he, Angus, had sat down and cried. Gordon had four of his upper teeth knocked out. Sheena got him to a dentist, who took out the stumps. (She posted me the bill.) A doctor put stitches in his lip. And no, she said, they hadn't called the police: 'We don't go much on the John-hops round here.' She told me not to come, I'd only get him confused. He was staying in his room for a day or two. So, his mouth – that's where I was – is sunken at the top. He works it not hungrily but like a ruminant.

New sneakers recently, new socks. Both of the old ones must have had holes. His beanie hat in the Hurricanes colours is gone; he wears a green one with a yellow rat's tail plaited from wool. His quilt is worn through so the padding shows. It's stained with mud. I'll send Sheena money for a new one.

Several years ago I followed my brother at a distance up Molesworth Street and Park Road and along Grant Road to a track leading into the trees at the foot of the hill. I had put on trousers and walking shoes, thinking I might have to slog my way up zigzag paths, but Gordon did not go very far. The track had barely started to climb when he turned off, using the chunky roots of a pine tree as stairs. He pushed aside fern branches and I saw him sink into a hollow as though going down in a pool. It marked a passing out of everyday life like the one he had made from our family; and made me hold my breath as though I were drowning. I might have called him: Gordon, come back; or: Gordon, don't go. No sound came out but, yes, I called those words in my mind. Coming to the tree, I heard movements at a short distance, heard him sigh heavily, with almost a groan, and understood for the first time since finding him that he had physical aches like other men. I had thought everything was in his head – and, almost, that nothing was there. I heard the shuffling of his feet on boards and the sound of his bucket as he put it down. No further noise then, except for the pines – never silent, pine trees, even in still air. I climbed the serried roots and looked through kidney fern. He sat like a gnome in the entrance of his hollow, or like a tired miner at the end of the day. He reached up his hand and pulled off his woollen hat, then took his thermos flask from the bucket, unscrewed the top, poured tea, shaking the last drop out. I knelt in the ferns and watched, wanting extra sugar for him, wanting every pleasure, yet knowing that even his way of tasting sweetness was changed from mine. I knew nothing about him, nothing of where he was – yet knew him best and only I gave him continuity and his original being.

The place he slept in on the hill must have been built by children as a fort or hideaway. They had carried in old pieces of 4x2 timber and a sheet of corrugated iron and made a roof resting on a pine branch and anchored in the bank behind. The tree bole sheltered one end; old patterned brocade drapes, probably from a rag bin, closed the other. The front, where Gordon sat, was open. A wooden door, tongue and groove, with the chrome-plated handle still in place, made a floor, which was kept off the ground by bricks in the corners. I could not see in. Later I discovered he had nothing there except his thermette and a cardboard box for bits of food. I suppose children still came, but out of curiosity, not for games. Gordon had nothing worth stealing. The roof kept out rain, the hill and trees kept out wind, and the raised floor stayed dry except in winter, when the cold drove him back to his boarding house. I saw he could be comfortable and not be bothered. He had his quilt and probably used his jacket for a pillow. I tried counting other things he would need, but did not keep on. For Gordon, I could not understand need.

When he stood up with his bucket, I withdrew: went out of sight up the path, then crept after him down to the road and watched him fetch his water from the fountain by the steps. I retreated again when he came back, then walked up the top road to my house and made tea for myself and drank it, eating biscuits, while clouds came up and the afternoon darkened and the harbour intensified its light. Gordon there, on the hill; Alice here. I began to know a sort of contentment – but only a sort. I can move about in shallows but don't dare step where the bottom shelves down.

I've visited his hideaway several times while he's away. I've thought of leaving a present – a few coins, a Snickers bar – but stop myself because of the fear he'd go away and never come back. Instead, I keep a simplified map of Wellington in my head and whisper it to him when I'm alone, as an offering: a hill marked with two crosses where Gordon and I live, and the only roads the ones he walks along, and the only places places where he goes, with Fry-up House marking the limit.

You make the rules, Gordon, I say.

Sometimes it almost seems enough.

But my life has changed. A hundred small things are rearranged and face each other in a different way. As for the larger pattern, it has shifted its parts, drawn them tighter and made room. Where Gordon and I once stood together, then stood apart, a third figure steps in from the side. Adrian, leaning a little forward, eager to see, arrives to join us.

Alice, Gordon, Adrian: we are three.

NINE

He wore a new pair of jeans to meet his grandfather. I was clothed in my usual way – and clothed in my belief that this expedition would leave Gordon untouched. How could anything – news of Marlene, news of a son, the presence of a grandson – penetrate the barrier of incomprehension his change of being had erected in him? I was not worried for Gordon, and anyway, Adrian would not get within talking distance of him. I had extracted his promise that we were only looking today. It was the boy who worried me. New jeans. His face shaved clean. But along with this care of himself came an aggressive puzzlement. He did not understand what was going on. I hardly knew myself. I'm rearranging him, I thought, but am I going to know him when it's done? Is he going to look at me and say: Alice, you're mad. Is he going to wash his hands of me? I did not think I would be able to stand losing him.

We parked in Aitken Street and I led him round the corner to a seat by the Backbencher Hotel. It was a few minutes after four o'clock. Now, in the warm weather of the last few weeks, Gordon is sleeping on Tinakori Hill. I imagined his schedule fixed like a train timetable in his mind, which meant he would appear in the next quarter hour, on the footpath over the road from us.

'You mean we've got to meet him sitting here?' Adrian said.

'We're not meeting him. He'll be coming past. You promise me you'll do what I say?'

'Sure. Sure.' He looked at the Beehive, showing its top – it's like the lid on a biscuit barrel – above the trees. 'I hope if he's in Parliament he's on the right side.'

'Right?'

'Left,' he grinned. 'If there's any left.' Grinned wider.

'He's not in Parliament.'

The girls from the three schools had gone. Some men I took for lawyers came out of the court and talked for a while on the footpath. High at the back of us construction workers in hard hats walked about in narrow places falling at the side. Adrian twisted around to watch. He had red marks on his neck where Bets had bitten him. How dare she? I thought; then told myself it was natural, and anyway he wasn't mine to protect. But he seemed mine, and that was dangerous. The invisible mending I'd done on my feelings was coming apart.

I pulled my eyes away from him and watched for Gordon; and knew from the way a woman walking down the footpath hesitated, changed her line, remade her shoulders, that he was there, walking up, a few steps out of my sight. I had a moment of incomprehension, a wiping out of normal sense, not knowing who would appear: Cyril with his quilt and bucket, with his eyes fixed on the pavement, or Gordon, smiling, six feet tall, raising his arm to wave at me.

'What's wrong?' Adrian said, looking round.

'Nothing, nothing,' I replied, and kept my brother to myself for a moment longer. There he was: scissored jacket, bucket, quilt, head on its perpetual forward slant. His vertebrae must be fused in that position.

He went behind a parked bus and I thought: Perhaps he won't come out the other end, he'll just vanish. I felt my twisting skein of grief again – chest, throat, head – and when he shuffled out and paused for a moment to let a schoolboy make a loop around him, I swallowed hard and set myself, and said to Adrian: 'Do you know that man over there?'

He was fingering the bite marks on his neck. 'You mean Cyril? He comes up Cuba Street, poor old sod. He's got no brain.'

'He sleeps on Tinakori Hill,' I said.

'Yeah, I know.'

He watched Gordon walk past the gates of Parliament. I said nothing, but let my silence press on the back of his head, and felt the little electrical jolt as he understood – like the shock that sprang between Gordon and me when his elbow joint was dislocated. He swung his head and stared into my face.

'Hey, no, Alice, you're not saying . . . Hey, no.'

'He's Gordon,' I said.

'You're shitting me. That guy's Cyril.'

'I told you he changed his name.'

'Why? How did he get like that?'

'No one knows.'

Adrian had risen to his feet. He breathed out a hard, half-accepting groan, yet acceptance of the fact that this man was Gordon followed like the closing of his hand. He took hold. He had no prejudice against down-and-outs. But how? He wanted to know how.

'No,' I said, 'don't follow him.'

'Why not? Let me go.'

'Sit down, Adrian. Or come and sit in the car. He's going to the place where he sleeps. You can find him whenever you want.'

Gordon crossed Hill Street and walked past the cathedral. I held Adrian by the pocket of his jeans.

'I want to talk to him.'

'He doesn't talk. If you've seen him in Cuba Street you know. He hasn't said a word to anyone for years. Except for thank you when they get in the way. He doesn't look at anyone's face.'

'I'm his grandson, for Chrissake.'

'And I'm his sister.'

We made a spectacle – an old woman holding a young man by his trousers, and with tears on her face. (I cry a lot lately.)

Adrian sat down and we were quiet. I dried my eyes and after a while said: 'Now you know.'

'How did he get like that? For Marlene?'

'And the dead man she found. All the trouble.'

'What are you doing about him, if you're his sister?'

I gave him an account of that. It didn't take long. I told him what I knew about Gordon's life since the time he had reappeared in Wellington.

'And you're going to let him go on like this?'

'What do you suggest?'

'I don't know. There must be something.'

'I've been living in Wellington for more than ten years and I've never found out what it is. Don't interfere, Adrian. No, I don't mean that. You've got a right to be involved. But Gordon's in a kind of balance. You can upset it like that.' I tipped my hand. 'Whatever you think, he's got a life.'

'Some life. Jesus!'

'Are you going to make him do something else?'

He lifted my fingers out of his pocket and stepped into the road, but Gordon was past the traffic lights and out of sight.

'You'll get run over,' I said.

'Yeah, by a tram.' He came back and sat down, moving sharply as I touched his shoulder. 'If you'd told me this stuff a year ago he might not have been so bad.'

'Do you think so? Do you really think you're going to make a difference, where I can't?'

'At least I'll be something new.'

'There's nothing new. I'm not sure there's anything old. Whatever he keeps in his mind, that's all there is, and nobody knows anything about it.' I stopped myself, halfway between lying and telling the truth, then said, half evasively: 'It's probably just a single thing. Something that doesn't move, like a statue, standing still,' and I went on, foolishly, that Gordon cast no shadow except the one pooling around his feet, and everything, past and future, contracted into that – a thought I'd once had about myself.

'You're talking crap, Alice,' Adrian said.

'Perhaps I am. Will you take me home now? Then if you want to get away from me you can.'

We walked back to Aitken Street, where he opened the passenger door – he always remembers his manners. But before he went around to the driver's side, he said: 'That guy who got killed in Gordon's yard, that would be someone called Cyril, right?'

'Yes, Cyril Handy.'

'So what's it all about, taking his name? I reckon he did it.'

'No, he did not. He was at work. Don't try and play detectives, Adrian. Gordon had his reasons, whatever they were.'

'I'll bet.'

He got in the car and started the engine. I made him use Thorndon Quay and Sar Street instead of Molesworth Street, where he might speed up to overtake Gordon, and perhaps cause an accident. (He drives too hard, too fast: young people do.)

I told him about Fry-up House.

'I want to see it.'

'Not today. And you'll have to promise not to go inside.'

'Why? Do you want to keep him to yourself?'

'That's a cruel thing to say.' I might have told him that sharing Gordon, in the last half hour, had brought me a kind of light-heartedness – or at any rate the kind of relief one feels when carrying a heavy bag and someone takes the handle to share the weight. It makes no difference to what's in the bag, and you're still attached to it, your hand stays clenched.

He said: 'Yeah, I'm sorry. You must have had a pretty tough time, Alice.'

How easily I cry. I hope it's going to stop when this is over – although I can't work out what 'over' means.

'One day, if you like, we'll go and see his place, where he sleeps. When he's not there.' I wanted to ask: How are you, Adrian; how does it feel to find this out? But it seemed intrusive, seemed coarse, and I waited until he stopped at my gate to say: 'I'm so sorry about all this.'

'There's no need to be. It's the facts, isn't it?'

'You see why I couldn't tell you?'

'Yeah, I suppose. The thing is, Alice . . .'

I waited.

'I promised Dad I'd find him and say who I was. I don't want to upset the poor old guy, but if I just say hello and talk to him a bit . . . ?'

'No, Adrian.'

'It can't do any harm.'

'It can. He's found a way he can survive. He's inside himself – as much of himself as he's got left – and I think it's so fragile. Any little thing . . . You can push him right over the edge.'

'How do you know he's not waiting for someone to get him out? If I just say: "Hi, I'm your grandson" . . .'

'No, no.'

'So, what? We just let him go on being – whatever he is?'

179

'Yes, we do.'

We continued between discussion and argument and I thought: I love this boy; and too, more easily, for love induced a tear: At last I seem to have a friend. I had not had one of those since Neville died. We ordered a pizza – I musn't let it become a habit – but he left soon after we'd eaten, saying that he'd promised to get back and let Bets know what had happened. I took that well because, if an old woman can say it, I've grown up as I open myself to love again. All I said was: 'Don't let her go and gawk at him, Adrian,' which made him cross and sent him away with too many emotions upsetting him, on a day of upsets. I worried about him driving.

We had not made an arrangement to visit Fry-up House – I mean, to stand in the street and look at it – or Gordon's hut in the pine trees. I did not really mind if Adrian went there by himself; in fact there came a settling in my mind when I thought of it, like the deeper settling in a bed when your partner climbs in. It was as if I could roll over and go to sleep.

Old age can be a blessing. I hoped Adrian and Bets would hold their conversation calmly, and after it be happy in that way – which I haven't forgotten – that blesses the young. When I went to my own bed it didn't seem lonely. I said goodnight to Gordon and slept as though I had company.

Christmas has come and gone. I thought, as I always do, of leaving a present in the hut – a bag of mince tarts, some chocolates with almond filling (he liked the flavour of almonds when he was a boy) – but, again as always, I rejected the idea, fearing he'd take fright and abandon the place. I come closest to knowing Gordon in his need to be alone – in his flight from contact with other humans. Yet there's more to his refusal to look in faces than fear. There's rejection. I'm the only person who knows that.

Adrian had the same idea – leave him something. I persuaded him against it. Bets said: 'We should ask the old guy home for Christmas dinner.' I told her he went to 'Room at the Inn' with all the other down-and-outs and if she felt strongly about it she could go down there and help serve the pudding or wash the dishes. They had me for Christmas dinner instead. The woman's no cook, but I don't complain about anything she does, or is, because she makes Adrian happy – frees him, makes him spark. She doesn't seem to open up deeper places in him, or he in her, but perhaps I'm not reading things right. They laugh a lot, touch a lot, and send each other glances. Although I'm not sure where their relationship is heading, it has gone beyond a boy / girl thing, which pleases me in one way – he's learning love – but worries me in another because although she has left girlhood behind, in most ways he is still a boy.

Maturely, he has forgiven me. He understands my reasons for lying. He makes in this a claim to know me. How wrong he is! I don't know myself. I've admitted, although not to him, all the things I've done, but I haven't discovered yet all I'm capable of.

TEN

New Year. What has happened? What happens next? Let me be calm about it – as calm as possible – and simply say what has gone on in these last two days. Putting it down will help me decide.

Adrian telephoned, trying, but not managing very well, to be kind: 'I'm at the hospital, Alice. Listen, take it easy, eh? He's had a stroke. We've got him in here. The doctors are saying he's pretty bad. Bets is on her way to pick you up. I want to stay in case there's any chance, you know, he might talk . . .'

There was more, a few words, commiserations, but my memory fails. I managed by doing things in order: changed out of slippers into shoes, put money from the drawer into my purse, checked that all the appliances were turned off, locked the house and waited at the bottom of the steps. I had not looked at my face in the bathroom mirror, the last thing I've done all my life before leaving the house.

Bets opened the car door like a taxi driver. 'Take off that old cardigan, Alice.' She's a one to talk about clothes.

'No, I'll be cold' – on that warm New Year's day.

'Sit there. Give me your keys. I'll get you a jacket.'

I put it on and felt more in control, and stopped myself from asking what had happened – she was outside all this – but when we reached the bottom of the hill and came into Gordon's territory,

I had to say: 'Who found him? How did you and Adrian hear?'

She slowed her speed while telling me. They had driven to Fry-up House and parked in the street. Adrian had walked past it before Christmas, but now he wanted to show Bets – and she was taken with the place (reaching out, I suppose, to grot and decay) and said she would come back and sketch it one day. She asked to see Gordon's hut. Adrian had been there and told her about it – the brocade drapes and floor made from a door. Now she wanted to see for herself.

They followed Gordon's usual route – Willis Street, Lambton Quay, Molesworth Street – expecting to see him on his way to Fry-up House. By the time they reached Grant Road, Adrian was worried. Late in the morning Gordon should be out and about. They waited half an hour in the car. Then Adrian said: 'I'm going in.' Bets, not to be left out, followed him.

'We found him sort of half in half out of the place. It must have happened when he was leaving because he had his bucket and his quilt. I've done first aid. He was still alive. So I went for an ambulance while Adie stayed with him. I went into one of those houses across the road and rang from there.'

'Thank you, Bets.' It's good to have people like her about in a crisis.

But at the hospital I said: 'When I go in to see him I want just Adrian.'

'Fair enough,' she said.

Gordon was in intensive care. For the first time since that day in his Ghuznee Street bach I touched him. 'Gordon, it's Alice. It's me.' I kissed his forehead.

'The doctor says talk to him,' Adrian said. 'But I'm not sure whether that's for him or us. Anyway – don't cry, Alice. I know how you feel.'

He tried to put his arms around me. Gently, not rudely, I put him off.

'I want to sit with him for a while. Please, will you go away?'

'Yeah. OK.'

'But come back, won't you? I want you to come back.'

'OK, Alice.'

I held Gordon's hand, not talking, but looking in his face. It was old and ruined but still held Gordon and the people he had been. Nothing was lost, but everything was turned about as he lay dying. I felt if I could say the right word he might slowly raise his eyelids – oh, the pain of it – and look at me. No meeting, no recognition, will repair our lives, but something remains that can be passed, an acknowledgement of who we are, Alice and Gordon.

I could not find the word, or words, but did not stay silent. I moved close and talked to him, saying: Alice, Gordon, over and over again; then Mother, Father, Loomis School, Loomis creek, myriads of places and names – and nourished and enjoyed myself in a curious way and momentarily wasn't aware of him. He made no movement, no flicker. I remembered looking at Mother's face before the undertaker closed her coffin. Father, beside me, said: 'She looks beautiful.' I had been thinking how ugly she became with her life removed. But Gordon, with life still in him some-where, retained a margin of beauty over ugliness. I won't describe him. He'd be a thing of bits, old and ruined and fallen to one side in all of them, but the whole of him, with his life still locked up inside – leave out beauty – filled me with love.

I murmured on, remembering us, until Adrian came back. 'Are you two introduced?' I said.

'Yeah, I tried. There's nothing there. But the doc says he might be able to hear. He just can't let us know he hears. I don't know whether I buy that.'

'Try again. Tell him who you are.'

He took my place in the chair by the bed.

'Hold his hand,' I said.

He obeyed. 'Hey, Cyril . . .' then turned to me. 'You don't mind if I call him that?'

'It's the name he chose.'

'Cyril. It's me again. Adrian, remember? I'm your grandson. I'm Adrian Moore. I'm Rodney Moore's son. You don't know him but he was Marlene's baby and yours too. Did you know she was pregnant? They never told you that. They told you she was somewhere else. When Dad was born they adopted him out. So he grew up without knowing who his real parents were. But he asked me to find you and say hello and give his love . . .'

He tried. There's no way of knowing if Gordon heard. I left them after a while and telephoned Sheena Gourlay at Fry-up House. She said: 'That's that then. I wondered how long he'd last. He's slowed down quite a bit in the last couple of weeks.'

I hadn't noticed it, and I'm the one who notices.

'Will you come and see him?'

'Is he conscious? Does he know anyone?'

'No.'

'So what's the point?'

'Yes, all right. There isn't one.' I had thought she might come for her own sake. I said goodbye and went back to Adrian and Gordon.

'Hey, Cyril, listen,' Adrian said. 'Hey, Gordon. It doesn't matter what your name is, eh? Remember this: "I have come to iron my trousers." Remember Nausea Bagwash, eh? "I have come to iron my trousers." Hey, Cyril, hey Gordon, can you hear me?'

I was astonished that the boy remembered that bit of nonsense I'd passed on to him, and filled with pain at his hunger for my brother to wake up and know. Adrian wanted to say: 'Dad sends his love,' and be heard.

I stopped him after a while and sent him away. I sat with Gordon for another hour, silent sometimes, touching him, cupping my hand on his brow; talking about our days in Loomis after that. Then I took a taxi home. I telephoned Adrian and said there was no change.

The next day was the same: no change. People came to see Gordon – some who had helped him, or tried, with food and clothing and money; others who were simply curious. (Gordon was Wellington's best-known street person.) Sheena Gourlay had a change of heart and dropped in, bringing the man called Angus from Fry-up House. I stayed out of the room, so I don't know what they said. She told me when she left that Gordon's rent was due and asked if she should keep his room.

'Yes, keep it,' I said and wrote the landlord a cheque. I told Angus he could have Gordon's bottle of sauce.

Bets took Adrian home for lunch. When she dropped him back she took me.

'I don't think all this talking to him works,' she said.

'No, it doesn't.'

'Adie just wants him to open his eyes. I know it's bloody garbage but he needs to say that stuff about his dad.'

'It's not garbage,' I said.

She dropped me at the hospital and drove away, very free with my car. I met Gordon's doctor in the corridor, and after I'd pressed him he told me it was rare for people to come back from as far away as Gordon had gone, and anyway, would I want him to, the damage that was done? I did not think Gordon could be damaged more severely in his mind than he was already – but in his brain, yes, I conceded that, and thanked the doctor for his honesty. In the room

I found Adrian murmuring still: 'Brahn boots. Remember that one, Cyril, brahn boots?'

There's no way back, but perhaps he hears, I thought, so why not try?

'Are you staying here?'

'Yes,' he said, 'for a while.' His stamina came from his need.

Gordon, I wanted to say, please help him.

'I'll come back tonight,' I said, and went home and tried to rest, but my mind kept turning over what I must do.

I sat with Gordon again for an hour that night, and telephoned the hospital in the morning. They were feeding him intravenously and helping him breathe with a respirator. The question would soon be asked: How long should it go on? When I rang Bets she told me Adrian was with him again. I said I would go in after lunch.

'You're taking it a bit easy, aren't you?' she said.

'Be quiet, Bets,' I said, and hung up.

I put on walking shoes, took my shoulder bag and walked the long dark paths over Tinakori Hill. It was harder than I remembered. My heart banged like a hammer and I grew dizzy, but after resting several times I came to Gordon's hut. A boy about ten years old was sitting on the upended bucket, wearing Gordon's quilt around his shoulders like a robe. He was pretending to be a king on his throne.

He started up when he saw me, and cried: 'I'm not doing anything.'

'It's all right,' I said, 'you can sit there. Just go a bit further away.'

'The old man who lives here is dead.' A well-spoken boy: private school.

'Not yet,' I said.

I took the photograph Adrian had copied for me from my bag – Gordon and Marlene at Barb's party – and fixed it with brads to the front beam of the hut, using Neville's tack hammer from his box of tools.

'What's that?' said the boy.

'None of your business. You can keep the bucket and quilt but don't touch this.'

'Why? What'll happen?' he said, growing cheeky.

'You'll go to hell,' I said. I don't know if threats like that work with children nowadays.

I walked down to Park Road and caught the Wadestown bus. What I'd done might seem self-serving. It wasn't that. I had made myself a step to put my feet on while I did what had to be done next.

At two o'clock I ordered a taxi to the hospital. Adrian said: 'God, Alice, you look shot to hell.'

'No, I'm all right. It's hard to sleep, that's all. How are you?'

'Getting hoarse. It's a waste of time. He can't hear.'

'Stay and listen to what I'm going to say.'

I sat in the chair. I felt clear-headed, although my face was numb as though I'd had too much to drink.

'Gordon,' I said, 'you can hear me. I know you can. Gordon, I'm Alice. Your sister, Alice Ferry. You wrote me a letter and I'm going to answer it now. I was good at knowing what you felt but I don't think you knew much about me – what was happening to me back then.' (My voice plays in my head like a record I can't stop. There's no word I want to change.) 'I was in love. You know about it – love, I mean. You loved Marlene. And you loved me. But mine was a deep black hole. He left me alone in there and I couldn't get out. I thought I was going to die. So I got in my car and I drove to the ferry in Picton and left it at a service station there. I came across to Wellington to ask if you could save me. I didn't think you could, no one could, but Gordon, way off in the distance, in the dark, I could hear you ringing like a bell. I thought: If I can get there, Richie Ayres will go away. I didn't say: Richie Ayres will come back to me, which was what I wanted. It was a little bit of sanity: Gordon will make Richie go away.'

'What is all this, Alice?' Adrian whispered.

'Stay back,' I said. I said to Gordon – further off in the dark than he had been then, but close enough for his hand to lie safe in mine – I said: 'I walked up from the ferry to your place in Ghuznee Street. Your "place", Gordon, remember? I went in through the iron fence, and you weren't home, and that nearly crumpled me in a heap. But I knew where to find the key in the bricks, so I got it out and went inside. I waited for you until it got dark, then I turned on the light and saw things I hadn't seen when I first came in – your table, your chairs, your coir mat – and that made you stand at my side. I even said your name out loud. Then I saw you hadn't done your breakfast dishes. You were never much good at housekeeping, Gordon. So I ran hot water in the sink and washed and dried them. That's when I heard the gate open and you come in. I heard your footsteps, and I thought: I'll be finishing his dishes when he arrives, and he'll tell me what to do. I had the door wide open for the warm night, and moths were coming in as it got dark. Then you were there – only it wasn't you, Gordon, it was Cyril Handy. And that was like having something ripped out of me – can you understand? – like having my chest cut open and something that shouldn't be there pushed back in its place. He had a cigarette butt on his bottom lip, as if it was stuck there with glue, and he said: "Gordy's sister," and he put one foot inside – in your place, Gordon, our place. I told him to go away, but he took off his hat and said you'd told him if he came round tonight you'd give him half a crown so he could drink your health. So I went to him

189

and pushed him. You remember your knife, Gordon, your sharp one for peeling the potatoes? I always told you you should cook them in their skins, remember? I was drying it, I had it in my hand. It went into him. I think I meant it to. It was hard at first, it went with little jerks, then it got easy, and he made a rushing noise with his mouth – I got his smelly air all over my face. Then his blood squirted up my arm. That must have been his heart, but I kept on pushing the knife until it wouldn't go in any more. Then I pulled it out. I didn't see him after that. He went back out of the light into the dark.'

Adrian's hands were on my shoulders. I was grateful for that. Gordon, my lovely brother, made no change.

I said: 'Can you hear me? I didn't look to see if he was dead. After a while I washed the blood off myself. I looked for bloodspots everywhere and wiped them away. I washed the knife and put it in my bag. I put the dishes in the cupboard and the cutlery in its drawer. Oh, I was thinking entirely without thought. His cigarette butt had dropped on the doorstep, so I picked it up and threw it into the dark. I wrung out the dishcloth and hung it on the tap. Then I put the key in the pile of bricks. He – Cyril Handy – was lying by the wall. I ignored him. I went out into Ghuznee Street and walked into town. I stayed at the YWCA that night and took the ferry home next day. Somewhere, I don't remember where, I stopped the car and took the knife out of my bag and threw it in a creek. Then I went home and lay on my bed for days and nights and lived in my head with Richie Ayres and I forgot about Cyril Handy. I forgot about you. But you wrote to me, Gordon, do you remember? Just two sentences: *I know it was you, Alice. When are you going to say?* As soon as they let you inside and you saw the dishes were washed, you knew it was me. Only Marlene and I knew where you hid the key. You never told them that a knife was missing.'

I was panting. 'And perhaps I left some smell of myself too.'

Adrian was holding my shoulders tight. I said: 'I didn't answer your letter. I tore it up. I put all that aside. And you went looking for Marlene. Were you also waiting for me? Years and years went by and I didn't come. I was happy with Neville, Gordon. And I was waiting for you. But you changed yourself into Cyril Handy. I didn't know that. And you stopped being able to look at anyone's face.'

'Alice, Alice,' Adrian whispered.

His was not the voice I needed to hear. Gordon lay still. There was no pressure in his hand and no change, no tremor, in his face.

I said: 'I'm sorry. I'm finished now. If you heard me, Gordon, it was Alice.'

I said to Adrian: 'I'm going now.'

'I'll come. I'll get Bets. We'll drive you home.'

'No, stay and talk to him. Try brahn boots again. Goodbye, Gordon. I'm not coming here again.'

I put his hand on the coverlet and kissed his brow. Then I went home.

I'm not bothered by what happens to me. Adrian will, of course, tell Bets. You tell things to the one you love. If she's the woman I take her for, she'll go to the police. That's all right, but I'm bothered by the damage it will do. I don't want Adrian to lose her.

Gordon will not come back. He didn't hear me. I was trying to wake him up so Adrian could say his father's name.

I am sitting by the open French doors with a glass of sherry. The evening light is fading and the last slow yachts are sailing home.

I saw his face a moment ago, smiling, but not at me. Adrian will be coming soon to say that he is dead.

Perhaps he opened his eyes and they looked at each other, perhaps they spoke – but I don't think so.

My name is Alice Ferry. Gordon Ferry was my brother. Father taught us how not to love.